"You wicked little brat."

As he spoke, Drew's silver eyes glinted at Marnie, but she stood her ground.

"I've never liked you, McIvor!" she challenged. It seemed inevitable now that she should have to confront him.

A smile touched his lips and before she could even grasp what he intended, he caught her face between his hands and pressed his mouth down hard on hers.

Oh, the devil...the monster! She even thought for a moment she would faint. She had to breathe deeply to slow her racing heart. "You bully!" she cried.

"You drove me to it," he pointed out suavely.

It wasn't true, of course. She couldn't have driven him to kiss her, because that was the last thing in the world she wanted—the very last thing....

MARGARET WAY

is also the author of these

Harlequin Romances

and these

Harlequin Presents

Many of these titles are available at your local bookseller.

For a free catalogue listing all available Harlequin Romances and Harlequin Presents, send your name and address to:

HARLEQUIN READER SERVICE
1440 South Priest Drive, Tempe, AZ 85281
Canadian address: Stratford, Ontario N5A 6W2

The McIvor Affair

by

MARGARET WAY

Harlequin Books

TORONTO • LONDON • LOS ANGELES • AMSTERDAM
SYDNEY • HAMBURG • PARIS • STOCKHOLM • ATHENS • TOKYO

Original hardcover edition published in 1981
by Mills & Boon Limited

ISBN 0-373-02454-1

Harlequin edition published January 1982

CHAPTER ONE

WHEN Marnie rounded the corner of the quadrangle, she caught her father and Drew McIvor in the middle of a blistering argument. Her father was shaking his auburn head furiously, his right hand slicing the air.

'I don't know how you could come here and *say* it, McIvor!' No respectful Mister, not today.

'I should, I suppose, forget it,' Drew McIvor drawled contemptuously. 'After all, what's so terrible about fleecing a rich man?'

'You're crazy!'

'Disgusted, Dave,' Drew McIvor replied grimly. 'You were one of the few people I trusted implicitly.'

'And damn it, man, you have every reason!'

'I did, but only just for a year.' Because he was very much taller than her father and facing her way, Drew McIvor caught sight of Marnie first. 'Go away, Marnie,' he said crisply, and he was a very commanding sort of man.

Never very sure what she thought of him, Marnie decided right then she hated him. Uppity, arrogant devil with all his damned privileges!

'What's the matter, Dad?' She ignored their most valued client and kept on walking. Her father's attractive, weatherbeaten face was thinner and sharper than usual, blue eyes sparking in anger.

'Do what Mr McIvor says!' The words shot out, harsh and peremptory.

'Yes, Dad.' Marnie raised her eyebrows slightly, but dutifully desisted, at least until she was around the corner. Then she flattened herself against the brick wall and listened unashamedly. Ever since her father had suffered a mild heart attack eight months before, she had adopted a very protective manner.

'How long had she been standing there?' her father was asking in a shaken, defensive tone.

'Seconds.' Drew McIvor had other things on his mind.

'I never want a word of this to come to Marnie's ears.'

'Excellent!' It was Drew McIvor's voice again, sickeningly upper crust and vibrant with disgust. 'What you tell her is your business, but I'm taking my horses away.'

'But damn it, man, you'll ruin me!'

'I made you, Dave,' Drew pointed out grimly. 'What's your feeling about that?'

'God in heaven!' Dave O'Connor moaned in shock. In a stable of twenty top quality horses, nine belonged to Drew McIvor.

'What made you do it, Dave?' There was bafflement in the deep, confident tones. 'Couldn't you have come to me? I've always had a good ear for your schemes—and your troubles.'

'I'm trying to tell you, Mr McIvor, I don't know what you're talking about.'

To Marnie's acutely sensitive ear, there was a shift in her father's tone, and Drew McIvor's reaction seconded her own dismal impression.

'The facts are conclusive, Dave,' he said curtly. 'Why would you ever bother to deny them? You've been systematically robbing me for the best part of two years.'

Robbing? Her father? Never! The charge was too preposterous to be borne. Her father was the most honourable, most honest man in the world. Why, all he wanted out of life was to work with his beautiful, high-pedigreed charges. She wasn't going to let McIvor get away with it. The monster!

Marnie charged around the side of the building again, the intensity of her feelings making her small, slender figure quiver in flight.

'Just you say that again!' she shouted, her enormous doe's eyes flashing with passion.

They both swung around on her and her father gave a terrible defeated sigh and put his head into his two hands. 'Marnie!' Drat the O'Connor quick temper!

It was Drew McIvor's hard hand that jerked her to a stop, closing on her shoulder. 'Don't you ever do what you're told?' There was a curious glint in his glacier grey eyes.

'Since when have I had to do that?' She shook his hand away furiously. 'I'm nineteen, Mr McIvor, not a child.'

'If you won't act it, how are we to know?'

His insolence took her breath away. 'I always thought you were an arrogant beast, but not a *rude* one!'

'Marnie!' Her father tugged ineffectually on her arm. 'Would you please stop.'

'And let him get away with his wicked charge?' Her Irish was up, and she jerked her copper head in Drew McIvor's direction so the thick, silky mass of her straight pageboy flew about her distinctive little face. 'What's he on about anyway? Let's have it out!'

'You'll have to excuse me.' Drew was looking at her with faint amusement. 'I'm trying to make it as easy as I can.'

'No, we're *not* going to excuse you,' she said forcibly, suddenly wishing she were a man. 'Tell me and save us all a lot of trouble.'

'Not at any price, Marnie.' He looked down on her coolly. 'I'll leave your father to do that.'

'Is it because I'm a girl?'

The beast ignored her, looking at his ex-trainer's wretched face. 'I'll have the horses shifted in the morning.'

'*All* of them?' Marnie's heart leapt in fright.

'I wasn't looking for this, Marnie.' There was a flicker of pity in Drew McIvor's cool grey eyes.

'Are you positive, then, of what you're saying?'

'Yes, Marnie,' he said abruptly, noticing how white she had gone. 'Believe me, this is the last thing I ever thought to happen.'

'But what's gone wrong, Dad?' Marnie was so beset with nerves she was shaking. 'Surely you can explain?'

'Ay, I could!' her father said finally, with a terrible grimace, and lifted his blue eyes. 'Would you consider giving me a second chance, Mr McIvor?'

'What are you saying, Dad?' Marnie's velvety brown eyes were almost black. 'Please, Mr McIvor,' she reached out in her distress and grasped the tall man's arm. 'Talk this thing over. There's got to be an explanation. Think of all Dad's done for you.'

'Which makes his disloyalty all that much more incomprehensible.' Drew McIvor suddenly looked hard and remote. 'I'm sorry, Marnie, I really am.'

'But you'll ruin us!' The tears suddenly stood in her huge almond eyes. 'You're an important man! Everyone knows and respects you. If you shift your horses from our stable, everyone will want to know why.'

Her father flushed darkly and bit his lip, but Drew McIvor looked colder than ever. 'Owners and trainers fall out.'

Marnie's little laugh had a wildness in it. 'Come on, Mr McIvor, they don't! Not you and Dad. He's won so many races for you. You're a rich man, but Dad's made you richer.'

'I'm sorry, Marnie.' Drew could be drawn no farther. 'This isn't really your affair.'

He went to turn away, but she swung on his arm, disconcerted beyond all measure with her father's grim withdrawal. 'But it *is*! Can't you understand that? Anything that affects my father affects me!'

'Ah, Marnie,' he caught her hand and held it for a moment. 'All I can promise is the racing world won't be given the real reason for our break-up.'

'But we built extra boxes for you!' For an instant she looked up at him like an uncomprehending child and he released her hand abruptly.

'I paid for them, Marnie. Believe me.' McIvor glanced away from the distraught girl to the father. 'Goodbye, Dave. I'm more sorry than I can say about the whole situation.'

Her father seemed struck into speechlessness, and Marnie shook his arm urgently. '*Please* say something, Dad.'

'I can't, Marnie.'

'Why not?' She felt so ill, she was nauseated.

'I have to see the books.'

'But he's leaving, Dad.' Marnie looked across the quadrangle to where Drew McIvor was getting into his silver Daimler.

'What do you expect?' Dave O'Connor sounded old and tired. 'When a man like that tells you he's been fleeced, he *has*!'

'Not by you!' Marnie's head was spinning like a top. 'Not you, Dad. You're the most honourable man I know!'

'And a stupid one.' Dave O'Connor squeezed his daughter's hand hard. 'Your old dad is a fool!'

'A fool you might be,' she said without even seeing the black humour, 'but you're scrupulously honest!'

Her father started to laugh, then he put a hand over his heart.

'What is it?' her eyes widened in alarm. 'You're not in any pain?'

'No, no, Marnie. Take it easy.' He used the same gentling tone he used with the horses.

'How much did he say he'd been robbed?' Marnie asked, already adjusting to the fact that something terrible had gone wrong.

'Thousands.' To Marnie's shocked, moved surprise a tear ran down her father's cheek.

'Dad!' She put her arms around him and hugged him, as protective as a mother with her child. 'You care terribly, don't you?'

'That's not even the worst of it. I have to give it back.'

'He's surely not going to prosecute?' Marnie's voice shook so badly it was just above a whisper.

'God, what have I done?' Dave O'Connor looked over his daughter's glowing head.

'Let's go back to the house,' Marnie said urgently. 'You've had a shock. You must sit down.'

She expected her father to dismiss the idea, but he only said quietly, 'All right, for a little while.'

They walked past the long line of boxes and Dave put out an automatic hand to a bright chestnut filly that thrust its beautiful, Arabian-type head over the door, looking for attention. Of all the horses in Dave's stable, and many of them were very handsome, Golden Rhapsody was his favourite. Not because she was the glamour sprinter of the season with an impressive string of wins, but because she was a truly beautiful individual, sound and courageous, with a lovely nature. Correctly mated, she would produce champions. And he had to lose her!

'Damn, damn, a thousand miserable damns!' Dave sighed painfully, because he rarely swore. 'Haven't I always said training horses is the toughest game in the world?'

'But you love it!'

Tiny Thompson, the wiry little ex-jockey who was now their trusted foreman, rounded the corner and Marnie shook her head at him warningly. There was never any need for words with Tiny and he touched his peaked cap and veered off smartly, his instincts as sharp as the horses he adored.

'How long have I been in the game now?' Dave was still walking, staring narrowly at the ground.

'Well, let's see.' Marnie put a comforting arm around her father's waist. 'You ran away from home when you were fourteen. You must have been a handful, because no one bothered to come after you. You spent the next six years working properties in the Outback. You returned to Sydney when you were twenty with something of a reputation for being able to educate horses; Bert Elliston took you on; you were there for the next ten years before you decided to come up to Queensland and start out on your own. You might as well say, your whole life.'

'News travels fast in the racing game,' Dave said dismally. 'How could I lose McIvor, my major client?'

'Isn't that what we're going to find out?' Marnie stared up at him. 'I always told you, Dad, you needed someone else but Didi to help you with the books.'

'But she's a whizz with figures.'

'A pretty dreadful whizz, if you ask me!' Marnie stared up at her father, her eyes big and dark in her pale face.

'The trouble is, I love her.'

'So do I,' Marnie said helplessly, 'but you must admit that apart from being able to do the most fantastic mathematical calculations in her head, she's the original dizzy blonde.'

'A funny thing happened to me on the way to the races. . . .' Dave tried to make a joke. That was where he had met Didi Palmer, an out-of-work model nearly fifteen years his junior. Love at first sight. For a long time he had liked to think of it that way. Didi had been, and still was, a terrific girl to be with, affectionate, placid, undemanding except when they were in bed; loyal, a hard worker and as obsessed with racing as he was himself. He the preparation, she the pay-off. Where could he place the blame?

'Why, hi there!' Didi came out on to the wide, open verandah to greet them, as pink and white and innocent as a small child. Past thirty now, she still looked remarkably girlish, and Marnie often thought it was because her most profound moments were spent with the *Racing Guide* and *Best Bets*. In the four years they had all been together, Marnie had never seen her stepmother angry or flurried or upset. Even when her father had had his heart attack Didi had walked around in an uncomprehending daze. But all that was about to change.

Neither of them had answered her, but Didi was still smiling. 'Aren't I lucky? Now you can both have a cup of coffee with me.'

'Even computers make mistakes,' said Dave, still talking to himself.

'What's that, darlin'?' Didi turned back to look

at him. 'I thought you said somethin'.' For reasons only known to herself she affected a Southern drawl.

'Sit down, Dad,' said Marnie. 'You don't look well.'

'Darlin'?' Didi waited for her husband to seat himself in one of the planter chairs, then she came to sit on the side, leaning over him. 'What's wrong with mah boy?'

Because Didi could be very sweet and kind, Marnie tried hard not to lose her temper. 'Just tell us what the devil you've been doing with the books?'

'*Davy?*' queried Didi, glancing down at her husband's bent head.

'Let it rip,' he said laconically, his voice a bit hard.

'That's it, Didi,' Marnie held her stepmother's big blue eyes. 'Speak right up and don't be nervous.'

'About what?' Didi looked genuinely puzzled, though this wasn't far from her usual expression.

'Drew McIvor was just here,' Marnie offered, helping her out.

'Well, why didn't you bring him up to the house?' Didi protested. 'Why, he's the best-lookin' man I've ever seen, and so cultured. Why, when I first met him I nearly forgot I was Davy's wife.' She smiled down at Dave's head and pulled it against her luscious, rounded breasts. ''Course you know, darlin', I'm all yours.'

'Maybe it was an accident,' said Dave, and looked across at his daughter.

'When you feel better, Dad,' Marnie said, 'we'd better step into the office.'

'Why?' Didi's face suddenly puckered like a baby about to cry.

'Marnie just told you, love,' Dave O'Connor stood up unsmilingly. 'One way or another, our sins find us out.'

'Sins?' Didi whispered. She knew there were sins, of course, but she had never committed one.

'If you'll just lead us to the office,' said Dave, 'we'll follow. Don't worry, Didi, as I'm your spiritual guide, the responsibility is mine.'

An hour later Dave was still slumped over the books, lamenting loud and long.

'Just tell me what I've done?' Didi wailed, all curled up on the leather chesterfield.

'Is she truly amoral?' Marnie asked no one in particular, 'because if she is, she can hardly be blamed.'

'I feel sick,' said Dave. 'I'm ill.'

'Oh, sugar!' Didi got up and rushed to him, the tears sliding down her flawless cheeks. 'I only did it for you. At any rate, what are you going on about? Mr McIvor has got pots of money. He's not going to die of anything if I make up a few little expenses. I was only trying to improve our standard of livin'.'

'My wife,' Dave sighed, and put his aching head in his hands. 'Let me try and remember that.'

'If you'll just tell me what I've done wrong?' Didi was uneasy now, but still fairly uncomprehending.

'You've lost us our best client,' Marnie said

quietly. 'Some people, Didi, object to being robbed.'

'I'm not in the habit of robbin' anyone,' Didi said stiffly. 'You know how much extra expense we've had. Someone's got to pay for it. You do all the dirty work, the hard work, and Drew McIvor gets to lead his horse back with all the money and the glory. Isn't he supposed to be a big business man with a finger in every pie? I think it's down-right disagreeable he should come here com-plainin' about his bills.'

'Really? You *really* think so?' Marnie was forced into looking at her stepmother very hard. Why, she didn't know Didi at all.

'What can a few thousand dollars mean to him?' Didi exclaimed. 'Rich men should expect to be made pay. I mean, everyone does it. Why, Jack Johnston was tellin' me about all the fiddlin' he gets up to. As a matter of fact, it was Jack who made me think of it.'

'Jack has been out for a year,' Marnie said pointedly. 'Wasn't that a lesson to you?'

'But he pulled a horse,' Didi said a little petu-lantly. 'But this is so unfair! You're usually such good company, and we're supposed to be goin' out to dinner tonight. I got that new dress, remember, and the cutest little mink jacket.'

'Better send it back.' Dave gave a strangled sigh. 'It's never bothered me, Didi, your I.Q. I knew there were lots of gaps, but you had this fantastic knack with figures.'

'Haven't I been a help?' Didi was hurt now, and

deeply subdued. 'I wanted to make you proud of me, and if it's easy enough to make a little money on the side, what the heck? Why, Mr McIvor should be grateful—very grateful indeed. When he started, owning horses was only a rich man's hobby. Now see how he loves it. I think it's very ill-bred of him squabblin' over his bills. We're only gettin' back the money we should have got in the first place.'

'Why didn't you know this when you married her?' Marnie asked her father.

'I've been happy,' said Dave. 'Didi is more a child than a grown woman.'

'Do you still love me?' For the first time Didi registered something akin to fear. 'I'll do anythin'. Tell Mr McIvor I'm sorry. I can even give it back out of my account. Won't even miss it, come to that.'

'Struth!' Dave groaned. 'How?'

'Well. . . .' For the next ten minutes Didi told them of the biggest plungers of her life. With her trick brain and Drew McIvor's money she had devised a system that over a period of eighteen months had raked her in a lot of money. 'Look,' she said, scribbling figures all over a blank sheet of paper.

'My God!' muttered Dave. 'I'm not ready for this. No wonder Charlie Kingston has been eyeing me pretty hard. Thousand-dollar bets!'

'I don't just bet with Charlie,' Didi protested. 'I've got to get the best price.'

'Tell me,' said Dave, looking over his wife's

blonde curly head to his daughter, 'are there any others?'

'N . . . no,' said Didi. 'Not exactly.'

'*Please*, Didi.' Dave leaned towards her purposefully.

'Nothing but a few trainer's perks,' Didi said cordially. 'I mean, we're all in it for the money. Owners and trainers alike.'

'Who else have you cheated, girl?' Dave suddenly shouted.

'Take it easy, Dad!' Marnie cried warningly.

'No one, darlin', I swear. There are only two of them anyway rich enough not to notice, and since old Hennessey retired he goes over everything with a fine tooth comb.'

'My God!' Dave sat down again, as though bereft of all strength.

'Perhaps, Dad, if you explain.'

'No.' Dave O'Connor drew a ragged breath. 'We'll give McIvor back what we owe him. He won't say anything. He's a man of his word. And we'll make it up to Dan in other ways. If we lost Dan as well, we'd be out of business.'

'If I'd known you were goin' to get so upset,' Didi said, looking at them both dubiously, 'I'd never have been tempted. I was just talkin' to Jack and the very next day they put the bank interest up—*again*!'

Absently Dave reached out and patted the top of his wife's head. 'Stop right there, honey. I'm more or less played out.'

'Are we goin' out tonight?' Didi looked back at

him beseechingly. 'I give you my solemn word I'll keep the books straight from now on. You're so busy all the time, you and Marnie. Don't you think I've been a help?'

'I don't know whether we ought to get a lawyer or a psychiatrist,' Dave sighed.

'What about a priest?' Marnie raised her eyes to heaven. 'I think it's about time Didi made a full confession.'

'Not likely!' Didi gave a startled cry, obviously taking Marnie seriously. 'You'd think I was a Catholic!'

'To what extraordinary church *do* you belong?'

'Leave her, Marnie,' Dave O'Connor bade his daughter tiredly.

'Is she bein' sarcastic, then?' Didi clung to her husband's arm, giving Marnie a reproachful glance.

'I must get back to work,' Dave pulled away with an involuntary, angry jerk. 'Heaven has chosen to visit upon me an insane child.'

In the end they did go out to their dinner party, Dave to try and escape his own thoughts, Didi because she had a new dress and the little mink jacket her two-thousand-dollar win on Past Reason had allowed her to buy.

'I'm the guilty one,' Dave O'Connor told his daughter as he kissed her goodbye. 'The funny thing is, Didi comes from a good family—on both sides.'

'There must be something we can do, Dad,'

Marnie said in a constrained voice. Dressed up for the evening, her father looked a very attractive man, just above medium height with a slim, wiry build, but there was a pallor beneath his weathered, ruddy-toned skin.

'McIvor would never be willing to take a chance on us again. Besides, I can't give poor Didi away, she's so silly and so vulnerable. Don't worry, McIvor will keep his mouth shut. I suppose he's already written me off as his only error in judgment. One way or another we'll survive. I have you, a great foreman and one of the most promising young jockeys in the State.'

'Ready, darlin'?' Didi came out into the hallway, so delectable a vision Marnie understood why her father wanted to save her.

'You look terrific!' Marnie responded automatically.

'So would you if you ever spent any money on yourself,' Didi pointed out affectionately. 'Why, a girl with your assets!' She studied Marnie's slender figure rigged out in a ribbed sweater with tight-fitting jeans. Slim as a boy, Marnie didn't look in the least boyish. 'Red hair and brown eyes and a skin like apricots and cream! You know how few girls have got that!'

Dave looked down at his daughter and for an instant his heart clutched in pain. Marnie had his red hair and very fair skin, but her beautiful brown eyes were her mother's. He was always afraid to think about Margaret; it stirred up too much pain. Margaret who had died giving birth to their stillborn son. He must have had a strange look on his face, for Marnie looked back at him anxiously.

'What is it, Dad?'

'I just saw your mother again.' He drew a shaky breath. 'Come on, Di. I don't have the faintest idea why I'm going!' He shook his auburn head.

'I *told* you,' said Didi, taking his arm and looking up at him with limpid eyes. 'Don't I look good enough to show off?'

Dave looked at his daughter and Marnie looked back. It was impossible to become too angry with Didi. Though she had had a high school education and that freak mathematical bent, in lots of ways she was just an adorable, slightly retarded five-year-old. No one looking in those shining blue eyes could fail to like and trust her.

It wouldn't do to ever let her in the office again.

CHAPTER TWO

THEY had only been gone ten minutes before Marnie decided what she must do. Once Drew McIvor knew the facts, and she would explain them to him very appealingly, he would have second thoughts about withdrawing his horses. All the races her father had won for him! She looked back at her reflection in the mirror. She looked

very pale and big-eyed. Her father had always insisted she never be too long in the sun without a
hat. He wasn't only thinking of her beauty either.
Queensland, with its never-ending sunlight, had a
high incidence of skin cancer. So her skin was
flawless. She scarcely saw it, mentally rehearsing
what she would say.

What if he were not home? She would have to
take a chance on that. Outside in the starry night it
was cool and windy and she knotted her long scarf
tighter around her throat. Of course, as he was a
foundation member of the élite with a river-front
home, she would have to cross town. No matter, it
would be hours before her father and Didi got
home. Usually they thoroughly enjoyed their evenings out and perhaps, even tonight, it would be a
mild sort of therapy for her father. Thank God,
Didi had had her winning streak. In a curious way,
she was even a genius.

The McIvor residence proved to be rather hard
to find, sequestered as it was from the rude world.
Marnie fully expected electronically controlled
gates with perhaps an armed guard patrolling the
grounds, but the long drive lay open.

It only took her a minute more to see she had
stumbled on the scene of a private party. Four cars
were parked at intervals along the curving drive;
comprising as she passed a white Porsche; a gold
Mercedes, a Jaguar—not McIvor's because it was
red and it didn't have the Daimler's crinkly
grille—and last but not least, a two-toned Rolls.

There was one highly painful moment when she

panicked, but sheer desperation drove her on. She would have to *beg* a minute of his time. Surely he wouldn't refuse to see her?

Her little runabout looked like a matchbox toy flung down before the Rolls. At least she didn't have to pay a fortune for petrol. She shut the door quietly and looked up at the house. Lights spilled from it, and music. Marnie had heard Drew had bought one of the historic old homes on the river and it looked fascinating with its deep, arcaded verandahs and wonderful lacework. Trust Drew McIvor to enjoy the gracious life!

Wide white marble steps led to the lower verandah and the front door and she could see the beautiful stained glass that had been used extensively around the massive front door. On another occasion such grandeur might have taken her breath away, but she was here for a particular reason and it wasn't a happy one.

She drew a deep breath, gathered up all her courage and pressed the button that sent subdued bell tones pealing into the downstairs hall with its magnificent central archway. What kind of a reaction she was going to get, she couldn't say.

Within seconds, a sober-looking gentleman with a face showing absolutely no expression emerged from a side door.

'Yes, miss?'

Marnie looked back at him, not the least surprised that McIvor had a butler. 'Would it be possible to speak to Mr McIvor, please? My name is O'Connor, Marnie O'Connor.'

'Mr McIvor is entertaining this evening, miss,' the man explained with something approaching surprise.

'It's very important,' Marnie said quickly, 'otherwise I wouldn't bother him.'

'You say your name is O'Connor?'

'Yes.' Did he have to look at her as if she were a naughty, if enterprising girl?

'One moment, miss. It might not be possible.'

I'll be damned! Marnie whispered to herself, faintly awed despite herself.

If that were not punishment enough, it was several more moments before Drew McIvor appeared, splendidly decked out in his entertaining gear.

'Well, Marnie?' He looked at her with a frown between his level brows.

'I'd be glad if you would listen to what I have to say,' she burst out determinedly. 'I'm sorry I'm interrupting your party.'

'Come this way.' He turned on his heel and now she was inside the hallway, following him past the brilliantly lit drawing room in which several people were seated to a beautifully proportioned library that was almost the same size.

'Sit down, Marnie,' he said as she hesitated just inside the double cedar doors.

She compressed her lips and looked away from the floor-to-ceiling walls of books. 'I will if you will,' she said, matching his crispness. 'I prefer not to have you towering over me.'

'All right, Marnie,' there was a hint of a smile

behind the mockery and he put his hand to one of the two deep leather armchairs flanking the fireplace.

'Thank you.' She tried to inject some mockery of her own, but it was difficult with the way he looked now. 'It's about, Dad,' she said, when he had seated himself opposite her.

'A pity.' He kept looking at her as if she pleased his eye if not his ear.

'You didn't wait long enough to hear the whole story.'

'And what is it, Marnie?' he prompted her dryly.

'My father is as honest as the day is long!' she told him earnestly.

'Did he put you up to this?' McIvor asked, almost indifferently.

'Of course he didn't!' Marnie was so agitated she jumped up. 'Dad doesn't know I'm here.'

'Where is he?' He was back to his very precise, clipped speech.

'He's out.' For a second Marnie faltered, deterred by the hardness of his expression. 'He and Didi had an appointment they had to keep.'

'So you've decided to take care of everything?'

'I've got to!' she said insistently. 'I can't let him live out this lie.'

'You love your father very much, don't you, Marnie?' he asked almost gently.

'Of course I do.' Because she was moved, her voice was blunt.

'Which probably would lead you, in turn, to lie for him.'

For an instant she was so shocked and enraged she couldn't speak. 'You couldn't be more mistaken,' she said, with a pained gesture. 'My father was only protecting Didi.'

'What *is* this?' Drew McIvor stood up as well, staring down at her intently.

He was so close to her, so dynamic, Marnie was confused. 'If you give me your solemn promise not to repeat it, I'll tell you the whole truth.'

'Melodrama, Marnie,' he drew in his breath sharply. 'I'm disappointed in you.'

'Please, let me tell you.' She swallowed hard on the lump in her throat.

'Little girl, don't bother!' The formidable, dark face looked grim. 'I can guess what you're going to say, and quite frankly I find it repulsive.'

'Do you think I want to betray Didi like this?' she cried emotionally.

'So your pretty, emptyheaded little stepmother is an out-and-out scoundrel. By the way, *can* she add two and two together?'

The shapely mouth curved so contemptuously— she had never seen anyone so good at it—Marnie literally saw red. Though she would later be appalled by it, she threw up her hand and struck him hard across the cheek, realising in a moment of sick horror that she had always had a deep, ecstatic urge to hit him; to wipe the mockery from his eyes, the sardonic curve from his mouth.

'So how am I supposed to react to that?' He

spoke quietly, but she could feel his mortal fury. His hands dropped to her narrow shoulders and he stood there staring down at her as though he had never before encountered her like. For once his air of unshakeable poise was awry, the marks of her fingers standing out clearly on his darkly tanned skin.

Nothing was happening as she intended. Marnie felt so agitated, so degraded and ashamed, she covered her true feelings with the remnants of her anger. 'Let me *go*!'

'Why, you wicked little brat!' His silver eyes glinted.

'I've never liked you, McIvor!' It seemed inevitable now, this violent, deeply personal confrontation.

'You've always been respectful enough, Marnie.' A cruel smile touched his lips and before she could even grasp what he intended, he caught her face between his hands and pressed his mouth hard down on hers.

Oh, the devil, the monster! She even thought for a moment she would faint.

'Now we're even!' he said above her with merciless deliberation.

She had to breathe deeply to slow her racing heart. 'You bully!'

'You drove me to it,' he pointed out suavely, not yet ready to release her flushed face. 'Don't get the idea I liked kissing you. You've been overdue for a good setdown. Think about it, Marnie. I've got eyes.'

'You can't expect everyone to like you,' she said
with bitter humour, so shocked and shaken she
didn't even realise she was leaning against him.
'I'm only surprised you would want to pick on a
helpless. . . .'

He gave a crow of laughter and released her.
'Helpless, did you say, Marnie? I'm almost sorry I
can't be around to keep an eye on you.'

'It's no use, is it?' She was ill now with frustration and despair. Why had she ever struck him? It
was so vulgar and out of character. Now all their
latent hostilities had flared into life.

'If you're so sacrificing,' he said ironically, and
leant back against the splendid, ornately carved
desk, 'why didn't you take the blame? I've never
been violent with a woman in my life, but I could
quite enjoy punishing you.'

'I would say that's self-evident!' She averted her
gleaming copper head and stared fixedly at the
rows of leather-bound books. 'What I've told you
is the truth. You don't know Didi. She's like a
child who knows no better.'

'Sit down again, Marnie,' he said kindly, 'you're
shaking.'

'I'll survive!' She transferred her gaze to him,
surprising the acute inspection he was giving her.

'So Dave let his pretty, irresponsible, childlike
bride handle the books?'

'Yes.' She had to ignore the hard, derisive laugh.

'That may be good for some people, Marnie,
but not for me.' He threw back his head in his
arrogant fashion. 'I've only got one thing to say to

you. Go home and we'll both forget you came here tonight.'

'No. *Please* believe me!' Despair drove her to plead with him. She wanted to go because she hated him for so insulting her, but he was about to ruin her father's whole career.

'Why the hell should I?' He looked down at the small, beautifully shaped hand she put on his arm, then at the creamy young face so near his own. 'Do you think you can make a fool of any man with those big velvet eyes?'

The effects of that kiss were too complex, too recent to be easily dismissed. A little experience provided some compensations. Whatever he said, for a few moments there he had lost as much control as she had. Marnie could still feel his mouth on hers, like a physical reality. Suddenly he wasn't just her father's most important client, but a rich and powerful man who might or might not be made to desire her. In the reckless urgency of the moment, it seemed like the only hope she had.

Her heavy lashes fell and her slender body swayed a little closer with an age-old will of its own. She was frightened because she couldn't trust him, frightened his tone had misled her. . . .

'Why, Marnie!' His voice was spiked with humour, and though his mouth twitched in the beginnings of a smile his hand came up under her silky hair and clasped her nape.

'How can you understand,' she said in a whisper, 'if you won't listen?'

'Oh?' His face had now acquired a faintly hostile

sensuality, but he was making no effort to help her out.

'I had to try,' she explained with an edge of frustration in her voice.

'I see.' His hand was still shaping the back of her neck, lifting and feeling the heavy silk weight of her hair. 'I wondered when you would begin to feel your own power.'

'I'm sorry I hit you.' She twisted a little nearer, not in control of her own subtle transformation.

'I knew how you felt, Marnie.' His silver eyes were half shut, narrowed on her face. 'You've been wanting to do it badly for a long time.'

'I have not!' She drew back abruptly, realising with swift clarity that he was hypnotising her, not the other way around.

'So what now?' He spoke dryly, still studying her drugged face.

'*Please* don't withdraw your horses.'

'And you're going to thank me?' He waited.

'You'll destroy him!' There was naked fear in her face.

'I'm not that important,' Drew said harshly. 'Other owners will come along. I'll be surprised if he tries it on again.'

She gasped aloud in pure anguish. 'You think I'm lying?'

'For the moment, that isn't my main concern.'

'Then what is?' she flared uncontrollably, her dark eyes enormous.

'The kind of deal you're trying to do with me.' The colour rushed up under her skin and she tried to pull away, but he held her, a whole range of emotions uniting them.

'If I don't take the horses off your father, I can ask anything I like of you. Correct?'

'No.' Marnie moistened her mouth with the tip of her tongue.

'*Yes!*' he said tautly, sounding very worldly and ruthless. 'I had the impression, Marnie, you were a very innocent girl.'

'Am I too young for you?' she said a little wildly, not fully comprehending what was happening between them.

'Yes, Marnie, you are.' He moved away from her abruptly, stripping away all her pride.

'Then you mean what you say? You're shifting the horses in the morning?'

'I'm sorry, I must.'

'So it's over.' She shook her head as if to clear it. 'At least never tell my father I've been here.'

'I promise you, Marnie, I won't remember anything about tonight.'

'Oh, you'll remember,' she said shortly, and tilted her chin. 'You'll remember whether you like it or not!' It seemed like a good exit line, so she spun on her heel and went to the door. 'What the devil——!' It wouldn't turn.

'Allow me.' His words hung mockingly in the air. He put his hand over hers and turned the brass knob still further to the right. 'A pity. You were the picture of outrage.'

Resolutely Marnie kept her mouth shut, grateful in the next instant she had done so. A young woman stood outside the door, looking at them both in surprise.

'Darling, we were starting to become concerned!'

Of course she was strikingly good-looking, with dark hair loose on her shoulders, and contrasting blue eyes. It seemed best not to risk an introduction, so Marnie nodded curtly.

'Thank you for your time, Mr McIvor.'

'Do I know this young lady?' Without appearing to do so, the brunette almost flung herself across Marnie's path.

'I think not,' said Marnie. 'Don't let me disturb you.' In a second she had flashed past and there was the butler waiting to guide her to the door.

'Thank you.' She gave him a brilliant smile.

'What an extremely odd girl!' The brunette's sarcastic tone followed Marnie out into the night.

In the car she started to shiver, the cold and the humiliation seeping into her pores. She had never had to beg for anything in her life; now she saw how terribly hard it was. Her father must never know she had made such a stupid, unsuccessful bid. All her life he had warned her not to take things into her own hands, yet it seemed to be an integral part of her nature.

Granny O'Connor, her father often chided her. *That's who you are!*

Well, that indomitable old lady had never made such a mess of things. Marnie's memory of what had happened in Drew McIvor's library was so vivid she shivered all the way home. How could she have acted so disgracefully? She cringed at her terrible efforts at seduction. What an amateur!

Nothing I ever do will surprise me again! She found herself muttering it aloud. The brunette's face had looked familiar. What was her name? Marnie was no expert on the social scene, but after a moment it came to her: Liane Maxwell, Judge Maxwell's daughter. All of them pillars of rectitude. Probably Drew McIvor was going to marry her. That 'darling' had come out so easily, she must have been saying it for a long time.

Tiny opened the gate for her, peering around the eight-foot-high fence as though there were enemies without.

'Where have *you* been?'

'Out,' Marnie said firmly. Tiny had been with them for years and he never could remember she was all but grown up.

'Atlanta's been playin' up tonight. I've had to speak to her twice.' Tiny leaned one hand against the car window, feeling like a chat.

'Is she all right now?' Marnie resisted the temptation to tell Tiny what was going to happen to Atlanta in the morning.

'Now that she knows I'm not going to let her stand over me,' Tiny laughed. 'If you ask me she looks as good a prospect as Golden Rhapsody. No doubt about it, McIvor's horses are always in the spotlight.'

'Thanks to Dad,' Marnie muttered, very bitterly.

'Well, don't forget, love, *he* does the selecting.

I'll bet he has a library full of stud books and equestrian manuals at home. Atlanta has one of the best pedigrees in the Australian stud book.'

'I expect Dad will have some news for you in the morning, Tiny,' said Marnie.

'Like what?' Tiny's smiling face underwent a change, and he bent his back a little so he could peer in at her. 'I knew somethin' was wrong!'

'Dad will tell you.' Marnie looked straight ahead.

Tiny lifted his peaked cap and smoothed back his neglible hair. 'Cut it out, Marnie. How in God's name am I going to sleep tonight, if you won't tell me?'

'Sorry, Tiny.' She turned her face to him and he could see the intensity of her expression.

'This news have a name?' Tiny looked worried.

Marnie nodded. She should never have spoken in the first place, but it would come as such a shock.

'Not McIvor?' Tiny blinked his pale blue, watery eyes.

'I'm afraid so, Tiny.' Tiny was almost family.

'No!' Tiny put his elbow on the bonnet to support his head. 'I know Mr McIvor well—a real gentleman. What possible quarrel could he have with us?'

'A private falling out.'

'No!' Tiny said it again, this time more forcefully. 'An intelligent man like Mr McIvor would be crazy to quarrel with your dad. Just *tell* me.'

'That's all I know, Tiny,' Marnie lied. 'McIvor is taking his horses away in the morning.'

'*What?*' Tiny's reedy voice positively crackled. 'Say that again, girlie.'

'Don't tell Dad I warned you.'

'Look, Marnie, there's got to be some mistake!' Tiny shook a stubby finger at her. 'Where did you get this information?'

'Right from the horse's mouth!' Marnie laughed a little wildly.

'I don't believe it.'

'Neither do I.'

'But they're good friends!' Tiny was starting to breathe heavily. 'After all, I've seen him thank your father in a thousand ways and he's never been short with a little present for all the boys, included. The last time was a case of Scotch.'

'Well, Tiny,' Marnie said tiredly, 'the party is over.'

Tiny shook his head as though he couldn't take it in. 'It isn't possible McIvor would set out to ruin us. I'm a good judge of my fellow man.'

'I know a few women you disapprove of,' Marnie couldn't help saying.

'It's bloody Didi!' Tiny suddenly burst out. 'Why didn't I think of it straight away?'

'Why, Tiny!' Marnie's voice was faint with shock.

'I told your dad ages ago he shouldn't let her fool around with the books.'

'Don't sing out, Tiny!' Marnie looked out at him aghast.

'It's that damned Didi, isn't it?' Tiny demanded. 'Always rattlin' on and asking questions.'

'Oh, come on, Tiny. She's my father's wife!'

'Come and have a cup of tea,' Tiny said.

'You come up with me.'

'Half a minute while I tell Barney.' Tiny limped away.

They were still talking in the kitchen when Didi and her father got home.

'So you couldn't wait, Marnie,' Dave O'Connor said tiredly. He didn't look at all well.

'Leave her be, Dave. I had to know.' Tiny stood up and pushed in his chair. 'A pity. A great, great pity!'

'You can say that again!' Dave's speech was faintly slurred. Never a heavy drinker, he had indulged himself tonight.

'Couldn't you tell him the truth?' Tiny asked, none too hopefully.

'And betray poor old Didi?' Dave picked up a kitchen knife and examined it.

'Just thought I'd mention it.' Tiny waited patiently until Didi came into the room. 'Good evening, Mrs O'Connor.' Tiny persistently called Didi Mrs O'Connor, although she had given him permission to call her by her christian name.

'Evenin', Tiny.' Didi gave him her big, devastating smile. 'How's the arthritis?'

'Worse from the shock!'

'I'm sorry.' Didi blinked at him, then looked around the table.

'Tiny knows,' Marnie told her.

'Well, I suppose that's only sensible,' Didi remarked presently, and put on the kettle for a cup of tea. 'We came home a bit early. Davy wasn't any fun tonight.'

In the light of events Tiny wasn't the least surprised. How Dave had ever married her, he didn't know.

Tiny had always been blind to a woman's fascination.

'So we won't work the horses in the mornin'?'

'No.' Dave reluctantly shifted his chair so his wife could pass easily behind him. 'To think I've been taken for a crook!'

Tiny didn't think it gentlemanly, but a real weakness to protect the softly humming Didi. 'What time did he say he was taking the horses out?'

'Oh, early,' Dave shrugged, and started to examine the carving knife again.

'Will you put that damned thing down!' Tiny urged him with a worried frown. 'We'll make out 'orright. It's a big setback, mind you, but if he doesn't say a word to anyone. . . .'

'Tea, darlin'?' Didi interrupted, looking across at her husband.

'Can't you understand what's happening?' Dave suddenly shouted.

'Hey,' Didi looked at him in amazement, 'don't yell!'

Tiny shook his head in complete cynicism and for a man with a gammy leg moved smartly to the door. 'Anyway, Marnie's got Jock Drummond's kid eatin' out of her hand. People come, people go. Jock might be persuaded to park a couple of his horses here. Old Murphy sure isn't winnin' any races for him.'

'Mmm,' was Dave's only comment. 'You realise,

Tiny, you're going to have to fend off plenty of questions?'

'Don't worry,' Tiny looked down at him kindly. 'Nuthin' will make me come out with it. You're the boss. I abide by your decision.'

While they all considered this gloomily, Didi asked with real affection, 'Would you like a cup of tea, Tiny?'

For an instant Tiny's wizened little face was a study, then he said politely, 'No, thank you, Mrs O'Connor. I gotta leave ya—I'm up at four in the mornin'. Ridin' work tomorrow, Marnie?'

'I don't think so, Tiny. I'd better stick around.' Marnie stood up moodily and patted her father on the shoulder. 'What's upsetting you most? Losing the horses, or the man's regard?'

'Both. I guess he feels the same. He really trusted me.'

'I don't know,' Didi sat down at the table very glumly. 'Anyone would think I'd done somethin' wrong.'

Whether anyone saw him or not, Tiny scowled ferociously. A woman like that would send him screaming to the madhouse!

The first float rolled up before the men were back from the track. Marnie had been given instructions, in the event that anyone should turn up early, to co-operate in every way she could, but when the driver thrust his ugly face out of the cab window and yelled at her to open up, she thought she would give him a bit extra to yell about.

'Where's your identification?' she called to him through the security gate.

'Take it easy, Marnie,' Kenny Mahoney, one of the stable boys, hissed at her. He could just imagine the sequence of events if Marnie wouldn't let them in.

'Are ya gunna open this gate, or aren't ya?' The driver, recently divorced, wasn't at all keen on women, especially ones who thought they were the equal to men.

'No, I'm not!' Marnie called. 'Not without the proper identification.'

The driver swore and got out, a burly six-footer with dark sunglasses over his eyes. 'Go and get your dad, girlie. He's expectin' me and I don't need identification.'

'Marnie!' Kenny prompted her. Both of them were tiny and this bloke was huge.

'Who sent you?' Marnie asked crisply, holding her ground.

'As if you didn't know!' the big fellow said jeeringly. 'What happened, girlie? Things didn't work out?'

'I want identification. In writing,' Marnie added, trying to picture McIvor's face. 'I can't possibly release valuable bloodstock without the owner's written permission. You do see that?'

'I can see one little bitty carrot-top tryin' to be obstructive.'

'There's a phone box down the road,' Marnie told him, sounding businesslike. 'Ring your owner and ask him what you're going to do.'

'Are you for real?' For the first time, the driver sounded flustered.

'Very much so,' Marnie answered him. 'Real and responsible. I refuse to release a horse without the owner's written permission.'

She looked so earnest, the driver took off his sunglasses the better to see her. 'I've been told, lady, this was all fixed up.'

'Not at all,' said Marnie. 'I know where I stand according to the law.'

The driver scratched his head, his small, deep-set eyes ranging over her petite figure. 'Go and get your dad.'

'I'm sorry, he's not back from the track.'

'And you're not gunna let me in?'

'No way.' Marnie shook her head firmly. 'I'd advise you to do what I said. Go and ring your owner.'

'I will, lady.' The driver shook his head like a punch-drunk boxer. 'I'm thinkin' he's gunna be real angry.'

Marnie just barely stopped herself from saying, *good*!

'What are you thinkin' about, Marnie?' Kenny came to stand beside her firmly, now that the driver had got back into the cab.

'Just amusing myself, Kenny.' Marnie sat down beside the gate. 'Mr McIvor is such a fine gentleman he'll want to do everything by the book.'

'Yah dad will kill yah!'

'I'll say it was you.'

Kenny yelped and moved away.

'Now then,' said Marnie, 'let's just wait and see what Mr McIvor has to say.'

Thirty minutes later, the men still hadn't returned from the morning training and there were three horse floats lined up outside the O'Connor stables.

'You've got a funny way of relaxin'!' Kenny said, as nervous as a kitten. 'By the way, where's your dad?'

'Oh, something has delayed them.' Marnie stood up blithely and shoved her hands into her jeans pockets. 'Don't worry, Kenny, I'm taking care of things.'

Several of the other boys were standing around in surprise and some alarm. They thought Marnie should open up, but she was the boss's daughter and a person to be reckoned with in her own right.

'Come on, Marnie!' one of the drivers who knew her called out. 'This is absurd. Open up!'

Of course she had to, sooner or later, but meantime she was going to get a bit of fun out of a terrible situation.

Just as the most intelligent and independent of the boys decided to approach her with a word of advice, a silver-grey Daimler swept up, parking its gleaming nose just inches from the security gate.

'Good morning, Marnie,' said Drew McIvor, as he got out.

'Oh, it's you, Mr McIvor,' Marnie said sweetly, beginning to open the gate.

'All the phone calls came as no surprise.' Because the gate was too heavy for her, he got hold of it and completed the job.

'It was very good of you to come.' She had to throw back her head to look up at him. She had never seen him so casually dressed, almost rakish, in dark slacks, a black polo-necked sweater and a short leather jacket. Even his hair wasn't as immaculately groomed as usual, curling like a satyr's all over his well shaped head.

'You're staring, Marnie,' he told her.

'You don't look—as usual.'

'I don't feel it. Absolutely.' He lifted his hand with cool authority and the first of the floats rolled through the gate. 'Where's your father?'

'Surely you've been told?' She spoke dryly, when in fact she wanted to kill him. A crime of passion.

'If I was, I wasn't paying attention.' He turned to look down his straight nose at her. Straight nose, curling mouth and a cleft chin. Handsome didn't say it. He had so much force, presence, like a charge of dynamite about to explode.

'Well, he's not back from the track yet,' she explained pleasantly, maintaining her attitude of deliberate non-participation.

'And he left you in charge?'

'Certainly.' The thrust struck home and she tilted her chin aggressively. 'I'm deeply involved in all my father's affairs.'

'No, Marnie,' he smiled remotely. 'I've thought of that and dismissed the possibility.'

It cost her a great effort to disregard the implication of his remark. 'I suppose we can expect this to go on for a while?' She gestured around her, not enjoying seeing how the boys had all jumped to their duty.

'It could have started half an hour earlier,' he pointed out dryly.

'Except I didn't see why we should be the only ones to suffer. You must be dead tired after your party.'

'No, I always find it easy to get up in the mornings, Marnie.'

'Hmph!' She made a scornful little sound through her nose.

'Surely you remember seeing me plenty of times down at the track?'

'Vaguely.' She should have said, *all the time*, but instead she told the lie. Occasionally he had even dragged some beautiful girl out of bed to watch the trials. Whether one of them was Liane Maxwell, she had been too far away to tell.

Atlanta and Summer Magic had gone quietly into the float, now Golden Rhapsody was being led out of her box.

'Easy, girl!' Kenny, who looked after her, spoke with a deep sadness in his heart. 'Easy.' Too heavy to ride racehorses, Kenny had won many prizes for show-jumping, as had Marnie. Now he leant his weight against the filly's gleaming side.

It seemed to Marnie that Golden Rhapsody knew she was leaving the human beings who loved her, for she was showing a marked reluctance to go into the float.

'Is it possible she knows?' Drew McIvor mused softly.

'Of course she does!' Marnie was so upset the
tears stood in her eyes. 'Horses always grasp at the
tensions in the air. That fool of a driver had
better be careful. He might get a kick.'

'What from, you or the horse?' Drew asked with
some satire. 'You're a violent little thing.'

'Ah, Kenny's got her.' Marnie drew a deep sigh
of relief. For a moment there it had looked as if
the thoroughbred might fling herself off the
ramp. 'Where's she going to?'

'That's my business, Marnie.'

'Oh well, drag it out,' she said shortly. 'I just
don't want to see the horses suffer from your mistakes.'

'You ghastly little brat!'

'Actually you're the only person I know who
brings out the evil in me,' she told him.

'Ever ask yourself why?'

'It doesn't interest me.' She put on her sunglasses to hide the tears in her eyes. Gay Chevalier,
an exceptionally good mover, who hadn't as yet
hit his stride, walked up the ramp unaffected by
the thought of travelling. If he went to a trainer
who didn't understand him he would never make
the impact he should.

'I'll tell you this,' Drew said a little harshly,
'they're not all going to the one stable. I don't
think I'll ever try that again.'

'If you were half-way to being normal, instead
of such an arrogant man, we could have sorted out
this dilemma.'

'Oh, I know, Marnie, I should bear my losses

like a man.' With one of the floats loaded, the driver looked towards him and Drew McIvor lifted his hand.

'Damn you!' Marnie said passionately, wanting to bite and kick and scratch.

'Why isn't your father here?' Drew looked at her angrily. 'It's an evasion of his responsibility.'

'What do you want anyway?' Marnie said, gulping, 'to kill him?'

'I've had about enough of you!' Decisively McIvor swung on her, then checked as he saw the tears trickling down her cheeks. 'Oh, Marnie,' he sighed with a tenderness and charm it was impossible to ignore. 'Why don't you go to the house? Your father will turn up—finally.'

'Thank you. Don't bother about me.' She dashed a hand across her cheeks. 'When it comes to knowing people, you're rotten!'

'Oh, I agree with you,' he answered in that uppity voice of his. 'I thought your father an honest man in a notoriously nasty world. So honest, in fact, I never bothered to check on him.'

'So how did you find out?' She whipped off her sunglasses, uncaring.

'Seriously, Marnie?' There was a twist around his handsome mouth.

'I asked you, didn't I?'

'Yes, indeed.' He glanced down into her tempestuous little face. 'I don't think anyone has ever spoken to me, Marnie, like you do. One dreads to think what you'll be like at forty.'

'Tell me!' she demanded sharply, doubly agitated because her father was indeed late.

'I was tipped off.'

'What?' she gasped.

'You didn't hear me the first time?'

'No one would know anything of our affairs,' she protested.

'Someone, Marnie, knows a lot.' He looked away from her and somewhat impatiently gave the signal to the second driver. 'Your father hasn't been at all wise.'

'But it was *Didi*!'

'I'm disappointed in you, Marnie. That's a pretty far-fetched story. The person I spoke to made no mention of your stepmother.'

'But the whole thing's crazy . . . incredible. Did you tell Dad?'

'Would it have done any good?' Drew glanced at his watch. 'Anyway, I had the whole thing checked out. You can imagine how I disliked having it pointed out. In fact, Marnie, all in all, I found it a foul blow. I picked out your father's stable when he wasn't at all fashionable, and at various times I've been asked why. First of all I was impressed with what he was doing with lesser horses and it seemed to me given class horses his methods could prove highly successful. Secondly, I found him a very likeable man. I knew, I *thought*, we could work well together and the results were quick coming. Unfortunately, hitting the big time made him greedy. It's happened plenty of times before, so why should we be shocked?'

'Rather, who's the troublemaker?'

'So you can vent your rage on him?'

'So it's a him?' Marnie remained staring up at him, amazed by his disclosure.

'Well, it's not a little old lady with a shawl over her shoulders.'

'There are plenty of them go down the races!' Marnie wasn't even thinking of a joke.

Kenny walked towards them, the corners of his wide mouth pulled down in depression. 'Pardon me, sir ... Miss Marnie ... could your dad have forgotten the time?'

'He's not actually all that late,' Marnie frowned at Kenny so he would go away.

'I know he wanted to be here when ... when it happened.'

'I'll check,' Marnie said shortly, infected by Kenny's anxieties. 'Go and give Jimmy a hand. He looks like a morgue attendant.'

'Yes, miss.' With so many of the horses going, the boys were wondering if they still had a job.

'Check now, Marnie,' Drew McIvor told her, not as cold-blooded as he seemed.

'I will in a moment.' She wouldn't allow herself to be directed.

'I'd prefer you to do it now. For that matter, I want to have a word with Deirdre.'

'Whatever for?' She shot him a dark-eyed, suspicious look.

'Simple manners. I have no argument with your stepmother. I've found her quite delightful.'

They hadn't even reached the house before Didi came running out to them. 'Oh, Mr McIvor, thank

God! Can you get us to the hospital?' Her lovely, transparent skin was drained of all light.

'What is it?' He went forward quickly and took her by both arms.

'Davy. He was complaining of chest pains and Tiny got him to the hospital. He's been admitted.'

'What hospital?' Marnie went slowly to her stepmother's side, her heart beating fast with sudden terror.

'Does it matter?' Didi started to cry.

'Because in the first place,' Marnie suddenly shouted, 'we have to get there.'

'Let's take it calmly,' said Drew, and gave Marnie a quelling glance. 'Was it the P.A., Deirdre? Who rang you?'

'That's it!' Didi lifted her curly blonde head. 'The Princess Alexandra. It was Tiny. He sounded upset.'

'We'll go in my car,' said Marnie, breaking out in a cold sweat.

'Mine is already out.' Drew McIvor stopped her abruptly.

'If anything happens to my father. . . .' she said desperately.

'You needn't say it, Marnie,' Drew said in a cold tone. Come on, you're wasting time.'

At the hospital, they discovered Dave had only given himself and Tiny a bad fright. The cardiogram was normal and the pains thought to be nervous in origin. However, because his blood pressure was a little high, the hospital would run a few more tests before they discharged him.

'The last thing I meant to do was frighten you,' said Dave, looking at his daughter's stricken face. Didi, so much more resilient, was carrying on a conversation with a student doctor.

'Well, you *did*!' Marnie's little laugh broke.

'Ordinarily I wouldn't have panicked,' he added, 'but Tiny kept talking about my heart.'

'Well, of course he did the right thing.' Marnie turned to stare at her stepmother for a moment but thought she must absolutely avoid a scene. What was Didi doing, fascinating the young doctor, when her husband was lying more or less helpless in a hospital bed? 'What on earth can they be talking about?'

'You can bet your life, not me.' Dave started to laugh. 'You've got to hand it to Dee—she's incredible!'

'And what about Tiny?'

'I told him to get back to the stable. He was all upset, poor old Tiny. It was really to please him I came to hospital at all.'

'He's a good friend,' said Marnie.

'The best.' Dave raised his hand and let it drop. 'Now don't go worrying about me. You heard what Matron said, there's no cause for concern.'

'There might be, if Didi doesn't let that poor boy get away.'

'Oh, Didi likes a little flirtation now and then,' Dave said tolerantly. 'It's inevitable. She's a very pretty woman.' His expression with its touch of tenderness grew sober. 'McIvor take the horses?'

'Yes, he did.' Marnie didn't think it advisable to mention that he was waiting down the corridor.

'It must have been terrible.'

'Golden Rhapsody didn't want to go,' Marnie told him.

'Did he tell you where they're going?' Dave picked up a glass of water and drained it in one gulp.

'At the present moment I don't care. Nothing, absolutely nothing, is important except that you're all right.'

'I'm afraid you must leave now.' Matron sailed up to them with a broad smile. A dedicated race-goer when she was able, Matron almost felt she knew the patient.

'When will my father be allowed home?' Marnie asked, not wholly in control of herself.

'As soon as we've run a few more tests.' Matron smiled at her. 'You mustn't worry, my dear—just routine. Actually it will be a great pleasure having Mr O'Connor with us for a short while. I like a little bet now and again.'

A ripple of laughter wafted over from the window and Matron spoke out confidently. 'Ah, there you are, Doctor Forbes! I believe they were asking for you in Ward Six.'

'I'd no idea!' Doctor Forbes steeled himself to meet Matron's unnerving eyes.

'Less than fifteen minutes ago.' Matron continued to give her broad smile.

It was all done so pleasantly it couldn't have been a rap over the knuckles, but the young man excused himself immediately.

'Now then, Mr O'Connor,' Matron said calmly, 'I think we'll take you downstairs.'

CHAPTER THREE

MARNIE, who had never sat in the back seat of a
Daimler in her life, was now discovering, to her
cost, that it was rather difficult to hear what the
people in the front seats were saying. Short of sitting forward and thrusting her head between them
like a child, she had to strain her ears to follow
Didi's abundant, noiseless chatter.

If only Didi had a clear, resonant voice like her
own! But placid, smiling, seraphic Deirdre had
decided a soft, breathy drawl was the most cap-
tivating of all, and to make it worse, it often
seemed like it was.

Even straining, Marnie had to skip several
words, then she heard Didi say clearly ... 'glaring
example!' Both of them were sitting up straight as
dummies, staring fixedly at the road. Didi didn't
have to do it. She wasn't the driver, yet she had
never once turned her enchanting profile. It was
almost as though they didn't want her to hear.

Perhaps Didi was making a full confession! In
which case, it might be better if they got her to
write it down. If there was this other person involved, nothing could prevent the story getting
out. No matter how one looked at it, it was a ruinous situation. Each time they pulled up at the
lights, so too did the remorselessly murmured con-

versation. Surely there was something behind it and this made Marnie anxious for many reasons. Didi wasn't a deliberate liar, neither did she regard the truth as sacred. In Didi's place, Marnie wouldn't have a moment's peace until she confessed her sins and begged for absolution. Surely Didi had a head start if Drew found her delightful? Nine out of ten men preferred a woman who looked like an angel—even women who made them suffer.

The green light flashed and they were away, vanishing around the curve before the other cars had even left the intersection. At another time she might have enjoyed the powerful, gliding ride, but she was headachey with frustration.

There, they were at it again, giving no sign of her existence!

Tiny was stationed at the front gate and he opened it smartly so they could drive up to the house. Marnie turned her face towards Tiny and gave him an encouraging wave. All the windows were up and everything was getting so much on her nerves she really might have pushed the wrong button.

Far from looking serious, much less chastised or repentant, Didi was behaving as if they had just come back from a lovely run.

'Are you all right, Marnie?' Drew spoke to her and she replied in an unfortunate, strangled tone.

'What do *you* think? Are you crazy?'

'It's the shock,' Didi explained, standing close to her stepdaughter. 'Sometimes there's nothin' to be done with Marnie, she feels things so deeply!'

'It's a darn sight better than feeling nothing at all!' Marnie muttered significantly. 'Thank you for your help, Mr McIvor. We won't keep you.'

'Are you sure you won't come in?' Didi almost begged him, anxious to make up for Marnie's rudeness.

Even knowing Didi as she did, Marnie was still profoundly astonished. 'I don't *believe* this!' she muttered, shaking her gleaming copper head.

'I'll talk to you at another time, Marnie,' Drew McIvor nodded rather brusquely. 'Thanks for the invitation, Deirdre, but under the circumstances, I'd better go.'

'You didn't *tell* him?' Marnie swung on her stepmother, filled with the feeling this was their last chance.

'Tell him what?' Didi looked the picture of bewilderment.

'Really, what's the matter with you?' Marnie cried brokenly. 'Don't you care about Dad? He's in hospital, Deirdre. It wasn't serious, but it could have been.'

'But tell me, how is it my fault?' Didi stood in her tight jeans, her tighter sweater and little body-hugging vest, clutching her two hands together.

'Wouldn't it be better if you dropped this, Marnie?' Drew McIvor looked at her with a flicker of distaste.

'And let you all destroy Dad?' The thought of her father lying in hospital filled her with an impotent rage.

'Surely it's the other way around,' Drew said quietly. 'I admire your loyalty, Marnie, but it's unforgivable what you're trying to do to your stepmother.'

At these words, Marnie burst out laughing; a grim, not a happy sound. 'What I ought to do is box her ears!'

'Oh, pet, you wouldn't!' Didi exclaimed, upset by Marnie's white face. 'We get on so well together. Why don't you come inside and lie down? Considerin' what you've been through, an' all.'

Drew McIvor was still looking at Marnie, thinking her quite capable of carrying out her threat. 'I'm sorry about Dave. It's all a matter of principle.'

'It is indeed.' Without another word, Marnie turned and walked dejectedly up the stairs to the house. Didi was still murmuring doggedly to Drew McIvor, but she no longer cared. Didi never meant any real harm, but such people were dangerous.

Ten minutes later, when Didi was still explaining how essential it was for her to keep Mr McIvor's high regard, the phone rang, and it continued to ring on and off all through the day. The news was out that Drew McIvor had changed stables, and for every avid caller both Marnie and Tiny had a pat, rehearsed answer; the disagreement between Dave O'Connor and his number one client was of a personal nature, and neither man was prepared to budge an inch.

'Tell us another one, darlin',' Harry Prendergast from *Racing Round-up* said disagreeably, but Marnie had to ignore it.

'Owners and trainers fall out, Harry.'

'Not when they work so successfully together.'
Harry sounded as if he was determined to get to
the bottom of the break. 'Why don't you put on
your dad?'

'He's got business to attend to,' Marnie replied
evenly. 'You know Drew McIvor, Harry. He's no
absentee owner, content to let the trainer handle
the horse's entire racing career. Everyone in the
game knows he's taking an increasingly serious
interest in the whole operation. That way, it's easy
to fall out.'

'You've got to tell me the truth, Marnie,' Harry
said. 'If not, I'll go to McIvor.'

'I think you'll find he'll tell you the same thing.
'Bye, Harry!' Nimbly Marnie hung up. If only
Drew McIvor would stick to his word!

'Well?' Didi whispered, cowering a little from
the incessant phone calls.

'He didn't buy it.' Marnie sat down wearily in a
chair and the front door bell rang.

'Let me answer it,' said Didi, absolutely forbid-
den to answer the phone.

'It can't be a reporter,' Marnie got up and
squared her shoulders. 'Tiny wouldn't let them in.'

An attractive, blond-headed young man was
standing on the top stair, and when Marnie
opened the door his eyes lit up with eagerness and
admiration.

'Hi there, Marnie, I had to come!'

'Oh, Ross!' In her depressed state, Marnie felt a
sudden lifting of the heart. 'Come in, won't you?'
She held the door open wider, and Ross Drum-

mond entered the hallway looking down at her.

'It's been a bad day.'

'Not good.' Marnie hung on to her smile. 'Who told *you*?'

'Dad heard.' Ross put out his hand and lightly touched her cheek. 'We were really quite shocked—especially since Golden Rhapsody has won three times in succession.'

Didi moved into the hallway and smiled a little uncertainly. 'Hello, Ross. How nice to see you.'

'Nice to see you, Mrs O'Connor,' Ross responded in his easy, friendly way. 'I just heard the news. I'm sorry.'

'It's not like Mr McIvor to be so disagreeable,' said Didi, and Marnie coughed.

'Let's go into the living room, shall we?'

'Feel like a cup of coffee, Ross?' Didi asked, catching Marnie's expression.

'Love one, if it's no trouble.'

'No trouble at all!' Didi gave her sweet, dazzling smile. 'Why don't you take Marnie out this evenin'? She's had such a terrible day.'

'Don't think you have to,' Marnie gave Ross a faintly wry smile.

'You know darn well I'd love to.' Ross lowered his long frame into an armchair, looking around. 'Where's your dad?'

For an instant Marnie debated whether she should tell him, then decided against it. Much as she liked and trusted Ross, the fewer people who knew where her father was, the better.

'Oh, he's around,' she said vaguely.

'I guess he's pretty upset?' Ross ventured. 'If

you don't want to talk about it, Marnie, we won't.'

She sat with her head leaning wearily back against the sofa. 'What's there to talk about? Dad and Mr McIvor fell out.'

'I never heard such a dumb thing in my whole life!' Ross shifted from his chair and nestled up close beside Marnie on the sofa. 'I can't understand, Drew. I don't think anyone has ever known him to make a move in the wrong direction.'

'He'll find that out,' said Marnie, 'taking the horses away from Dad.'

'Could be Dad might want to have a talk to your father.' Ross tried to cheer her up. 'He's sure looking for a new trainer. Murphy seems to have lost the old magic.'

'He's really very capable,' Marnie said fairly. 'Dad has been lucky managing McIvor's horses. All of them have been swans.'

'Well, we've got one or two promising gallopers,' Ross slid his arm along the back of the sofa, so it was curled around Marnie's shoulders. 'It's possible your dad could get a lot more out of them than Tom. One of the snags is what Drew's going to say about the split. Dad thinks the world of him. In fact, I think he's been on to him already.'

This piece of news made Marnie's stomach lurch. Believing her father to be a cheat and a liar, how could Drew McIvor recommend the stable? Prospective clients would now avoid them like the plague.

Didi came back with the coffee and immediately
Marnie led the conversation away from horses
altogether. There was nothing anyone could do
now but wait and see how McIvor reacted. Much
as he incited her, none better, she realised she was
counting on one certainty: he wasn't a vindictive
man.

A couple of hours later, as Marnie was putting the
finishing touches to her make-up, Didi put her
head around the door.

'Would you like to wear my jacket?' She was
clutching the ravishing little fur, her big blue eyes
appealing to Marnie to understand.

'Oh, Didi!' Marnie shook her head.

'Please, darlin', *please* wear it,' Didi whispered.
'I know you're cross with me, but if I owned up and
told Mr McIvor, everyone would be laughin' at
me. I couldn't go anywhere that they wouldn't be
laughin' and talkin'.'

'He wouldn't have told anyone,' Marnie
answered quietly.

'I'm a coward, Marnie!' The tears suddenly
rolled down Didi's face. 'I'm not spunky and
special like you. People have got to *like* me!'

'Everyone does!' Marnie felt a spasm of pity.
'You never thought, Didi, of the results of all this
fiddlin', as you call it?'

'I never thought Mr McIvor would make a fuss.'
Didi held the fur under her chin like a protection.
'I've heard time an' time again, he's one of the
richest men in the State.'

'It's as much the same for a rich man to be robbed.'

'No, it's not!' Didi countered, very vehemently for her. 'Look at Robin Hood. He was a hero!'

'Robin Hood?' gasped Marnie.

'What's the matter with your voice?' queried Didi. 'You sound strange.'

'I don't think I want to go,' Marnie said.

'Oh, do!' Didi urged her. 'It's lovely to go out to dinner and some dancin' when you're feelin' low.'

'Just see you leave that phone off the hook,' Marnie warned, and slipped into her dress. 'I don't think anyone would bother you, but you never know.'

'Did they have to mention it on the news?' Didi winced.

'Just wait for the morning paper.' Marnie sought out her evening shoes, packed away in their box. 'One way or another, McIvor is never out of it.'

'I'm so depressed,' Didi moaned. 'I think I'll go and see Dave.'

'You know he told you not to,' Marnie turned round to the mirror. 'Is this dress good enough? Ross mentioned something about trying to get in to Ricco's.'

Didi whistled. 'That will cost him a packet!'

'I'm certain his father doesn't keep him short,' Marnie said a little tartly. Ross was in his final year studying Law and certain of a good future with his father's long-established law firm.

'You know he's in love with you,' Didi said dreamily, circling Marnie's petite figure.

'I'm sure his family have already got some nice girl picked out,' shrugged Marnie.

'She couldn't be a patch on you!' Didi said sincerely. 'Why, a girl like you has it all sewn up. Please wear my fur. It will give you that final touch.'

With Didi pressing it on her so pleadingly, Marnie had no option. Ordinarily she would have jumped at the offer, but now she linked the beautiful mink with Didi's misdemeanours.

'Honestly,' Didi said more happily, 'you have skin like a pearl. Which makes me think, you should wear mine.'

'Oh no, Didi, this necklace looks all right.'

'If you're going to Ricco's. . . .' Didi went off; a woman who took dressing up very seriously.

Left alone for a moment, Marnie stared in the mirror. She seldom bothered much with make-up, having a beautiful skin, but she had to admit that colour on the face made an enormous difference. Her eyes were huge, her brows and lashes darkened, eyelids softly shadowed and her skin with a light foundation on it really did glisten like a pearl. Normally she never wore bright colour on her mouth; now you could see its shape—soft and full and tender. Her face wasn't a classic oval like Didi's, but rather wide at the jawline. There had been a time when she had hated her red hair and brown eyes that everyone said tilted up at the corners like a cat's, now her unusual looks seemed a decided plus.

'Here we are!' Didi was back, dropping the long

string of pearls with its beautiful clasp over
Marnie's head. 'It's interestin' the way pearls have
come back into fashion. Crazy, too, they ever went
out. They're so flatterin'.'

'Aren't they?' A little dazedly Marnie fingered
the almost waist-length string. At least they had
been come by honestly. Her father had bought
them for Didi at an auction of Georgian and Vic-
torian jewellery after a big win. Her dress was a
tobacco silk with a camisole top and its own blazer
and against the silk the pearl rope contrasted
beautifully.

'You'll do!' said Didi, and held out the mink
jacket. 'It's put me in a good mood again, seein'
you all dressed up.'

It put Ross into a good mood too. His hazel,
gold-flecked eyes lit up and he wondered yet again
why Marnie didn't know she was so beautiful. It
made his heart beat irregularly just to look at her.
That she had gone to so much trouble to dress up
pleased him too. His mother and two sisters were
very fashion-conscious, so he had come to expect
that *the* girl in his life should be immaculately
turned out. The one thing that had troubled him a
little about Marnie was her lack of interest in
clothes, even if she wore jeans and a T-shirt with a
lot of dash.

It was dreamlike, their entrance into the very
swanky Ricco's. The reaction pleased Ross. Plenty
of eyes studied Marnie with that gorgeous red hair
and fawn's eyes and the packaging was superb
even if the delicious little fur jacket was her step-

mother's. Ross's intellectual mother found Didi a 'perfect fool', but Ross quite liked her. She was luscious to look at and if she never said anything very perceptive or profound, she never said anything hurtful either. Which was more than could be said for his mother.

Marnie, walking half the length of the discreetly lit room, saw Drew McIvor first. Those startling light eyes had been instantly on her, concentrating on the mink and the pearls.

Despite herself she flushed, and he treated her to a tight smile. Probably he thought he had bought them. She wished fervently she had never worn them.

'Oh, there's Drew!' said Ross, following her gaze.

'I don't want to speak to him,' Marnie said quietly. 'I can't.'

'Oh, gosh!' Ross felt a little unnerved. He had always admired his father's friend and been flattered by the older man's interest in him and his studies, now Marnie was asking him to ignore a family friend.

As it happened, Drew McIvor decided by getting to his feet as they approached his table.

'How are you, Marnie ... Ross?' The handsome mouth smiled charmingly.

'Fine, thanks, Drew.' Ross followed his instincts and smiled and shook the older man's hand. 'Oh, hello there, Miss Maxwell.'

'Ross,' Liane Maxwell responded, just curving her finely cut lips. 'Surely our mysterious young lady is Miss O'Connor?'

'Who else has red hair?' said Marnie, and

though Ross was still standing, smiling like a perfect simpleton, she started to move.

'Enjoy yourselves,' said Ross, unable to think of anything else. He too moved away after Marnie and the waiter thinking Marnie could have been a little more gracious. *Mysterious lady*—what had that meant?

They were no sooner seated, fenced around by their menus, when Ross asked the question.

'Do you know what she meant?'

Marnie shook her head, so hot under her skin she felt she was on fire. 'Of all the nights to come here!' she muttered.

'Don't you like it?' Ross exclaimed, upset at the thought.

'Oh, it's lovely!' Marnie looked up at him apologetically, her velvety eyes dark with agitation. 'It's just that I never expected to see Drew McIvor.'

'He dines out a lot,' said Ross, taking hold of her hand. 'If his being here upsets you, we'll leave.'

'How can we?' Marnie was so shaken she was considering the suggestion.

'We can't really.' Ross detested scenes. 'But if you want to, we will.'

It was impossible to ignore the disappointment in his voice. 'At least he's got his back to us,' Marnie tried for a reassuring smile. 'I guess I just panicked for a minute.'

'Poor little thing!' Ross had no idea why. 'In any case, he was very nice. Have you met *her* before?'

'I've seen her,' Marnie said slowly. 'How I wish they weren't here!'

'Have a glass of champagne,' Ross suggested.

'Something imported and expensive.' He gave her a smile of great appeal and she responded by laughing.

'I'm not usually so difficult.'

'You're upset,' Ross said quietly. 'That's why I wanted us to come out and celebrate!' Because he really wanted to hold her in his arms, he added gaily, 'While we're waiting for someone to take the order, let's dance.'

He stood up, and Marnie, feeling overheated with her silk blazer on, slipped out of it, showing her lovely white shoulders and the full glory of the pearls. She couldn't see but she could feel pairs of eyes boring into her and she was grateful at least that she didn't have a well-known face like Liane Maxwell. Time enough for people to talk about her: *Dave O'Connor's* daughter.

By the time they were half way through a truly superb meal she was fairly relaxed.

'No sweet—no, I couldn't!'

'I think I will.' Still at the unfillable stage, Ross decided on an elaborate dessert, ruinous with calories. 'Perfect,' he said solemnly, when he had finished it. 'You should have had some.'

'I loved watching you. You're a very happy person, aren't you, Ross?'

'Aren't *you*?' He sounded surprised. 'You're usually so gay, such fun to be with. Surely you're happy too?'

'I don't believe I am.' Thinking it, she knew it was true.

'You work so hard for your father.'

'I enjoy it.' Instantly she was intensely loyal.

'Okay, sweetie, take it easy. I only mean compared to say, my sisters, you have a hard life. Up so early, always on the go. Then you have your own show riding. No wonder you can never put on a pound.' His sisters, for instance, never stopped talking about diets. 'Come on,' Ross stood up and went around to her, 'I have to dance this off.'

He wasn't at all a good dancer, Marnie had long since decided, but he always acted so enormously pleased with himself and life that Marnie's liking was growing into a real affection. A person like Ross could never overwhelm her, and he could give her so much.

She was relaxing dreamily in his arms when a woman's clear voice spoke up from behind her.

'Here we are again!'

Marnie turned her head, wondering why Liane Maxwell was anxious to meet her. *Why?*

'Won't you both join us for coffee?' Liane smiled charmingly over Drew McIvor's broad shoulder. 'Do say yes!'

Ross didn't know what to say and just as he was drawing a ragged breath, Marnie said pleasantly: 'How kind!' Whatever it cost her she wasn't going to be intimidated by a mere society butterfly. She could even, if she had the available minute, ask Drew McIvor what he intended to tell Jock Drummond. It would be hard enough trying to get to sleep without worrying if McIvor had turned away a prospective client from her father's stable.

'This is really too much, isn't it?' Liane Maxwell

smiled when they were all seated at the one table. 'The truth is, my dear, I would have thought you'd be too upset to dine out tonight.'

'Why don't we just stop talking about it, Liane?' Drew said quietly.

'Oh, I'm sorry, darling!' Liane pulled a face of mock hurt. 'I'll be as sympatico as I can.'

'You're not sympatico at all,' said Marnie.

'I understand why Ross likes dancing with you, Marnie,' Drew stood up and put a hand on Marnie's arm. 'You move beautifully.'

And that did seem to be true, for they were very swiftly on the floor.

'Your lady friend is a bitch,' she told McIvor decisively. 'She likes hurting people.'

'She's hardly ever like that,' he replied blandly.

'She's got to know *everything*, doesn't she?'

'She doesn't, Marnie,' he looked down into her stormy face. 'How's your father?'

'Do you care?'

He held her closer and her eyes widened. 'Resting quietly. We don't know the results of the tests yet.'

'I've a sneaking suspicion, Marnie, he never put you across his knee,' Drew told her.

'I'll tell you something, Mr McIvor,' she said bluntly, 'he never had to.'

'You mean it's only recently you've started to misbehave?'

She raised her head to look up into his face and as she did so he bent his to continue his inspection.

'Well?' she challenged him, a fluttering inside of her.

'I've never seen you dressed up for the evening.'

'I'm glad. You're very critical.'

'You don't understand that you're beautiful?'

'No—you're quite wrong.' She was trembling now, her heart pounding. 'I've actually got quite a funny face. My eyes are too big, and my mouth.'

'They give your face distinction. You don't look like anybody else. I could wish for you a nicer *nature*,' he added.

'Let's not dance any more.' She couldn't cope with him, nor communicate, the trembling he induced in her a shrieking madness.

'You don't like me a lot, do you, Marnie?' he said.

'That we already know.'

'I could easily make you.'

'What monstrous vanity!' There were moments when she hated herself for all kinds of things, now she hated herself for feeling this pulsing excitement. No one else she had ever known or seen, except on the silver screen, exuded such male sexuality, and it was positively unnerving. 'I don't have a reason in the world for speaking to you at all,' she added crisply, and it made her feel better.

'Not even to ask me what I told Jock Drummond?'

His tone of voice, so worldly and mocking, made her go weak with alarm. 'Would you consider telling me?' she asked him, looking up briefly into his grey eyes.

'I didn't think I could improve on *your* bulletin, Marnie.'

'Please tell me the truth.' On impulse she tightened her hold on his hand.

'I'm visiting friends at the Coast on Sunday—do you want to come?'

'*What?*' She stared up at him with a little frown, her eyes revealing her disbelief.

'What else are you doing?' he asked.

'Surely you're not finding me attractive?'

'Oh, come on, Marnie,' he smiled down at her. 'I'm just wondering what's to become of you at this rate. Fiery, prickly little thing, openly contemptuous. Keep it up, little one, and you'll end up all alone.'

'I'm sure you're right,' she answered tartly, without thinking. 'Tell me, are you proposing to act father confessor?'

'Touché!' he burst into a low laugh. 'But stop right there, Marnie.'

What a fool I am, she reproached herself, exhilarated with their exchanges. 'What *did* you tell Mr Drummond?' she insisted.

'Are you coming?'

'The whole thing seems a little strange.'

'You can relay a message to your father.'

This time she had to be very careful. 'Gladly,' she said quietly.

'Don't try *anything* any more. One false move and I'll come out with the whole story. Jock Drummond is my friend. I know your father will understand perfectly.'

'Who knows, some day you might as well.' Her entire body was weak and shaking. She knew what her father was, how good he was. Still, he would have to bear the responsibility for Drew.

'Please may we go back to the table, I want to go home.'

'You still haven't answered me,' Drew stated decisively.

She tilted her head to examine his face carefully. It would be so terribly easy to become emotionally involved with this man. He knew it and she knew it, so what idea was he working on?

'Why do you want me to come?' she asked.

'Because I'm convinced you need a little relaxation. It's rather a hard sort of existence you have, Marnie. I know how hard you work.'

'I've also got lots of friends.'

'Are you aware Ross's mother has his future wife picked out for him?'

'You're joking!' She lifted her head to find his silver eyes steadily on hers.

'Ah, mothers!' he said. 'The information, Marnie for what it's worth, is reliable. I've met her, she's a very pretty girl and Ross sees a lot of her.'

'There's nothing strange about that. He's a bachelor. I wonder how Miss Maxwell would feel if she knew you were chatting up me.'

'Am I?' he laughed, a very attractive, disturbing sound.

'It seems remarkably like it.'

'No such thing. You're a child.'

A child who was acutely aware of her body. And his.

'So I'll pass up your kind offer.'

'No, you won't!'

'That sounds like a threat,' she said uneasily.

'No, I'm just accustomed to getting my own way.' The music stopped and his hand dropped to her waist, guiding her gently off the floor. 'I'll pick you up outside your front gate at eight-thirty sharp.'

They were back at the table and Ross stood up with a smile that didn't move to his eyes. 'I didn't think either of you were coming back.'

'Oh, we quite enjoy talking.'

'You seem to be good at it!' Liane looked a little angry and it showed in her tone. 'Is that why you visited Drew at his home, to talk him out of sacking your father?'

'On the contrary, Drew and I are good friends.'

'Take note.' For an instant there was a sardonic sparkle in Drew's eyes.

'I don't feel as though I want to stay any longer.' Liane looked ready to tip over the centrepiece of flowers.

'You must talk to Miss Maxwell,' Marnie said calmly, 'and tell her not to be impolite to her *invited* guests!'

'*Please*, Marnie,' Ross protested feebly. Liane Maxwell, after all, was Judge Maxwell's daughter. One day he might have to come up before him.

'You're quite right. *Bon appetit!*' She darted up with swift grace, the very picture of devilment. 'It's quite possible if I leave, Drew will pay some attention to you.'

'Why, the cheek!' Liane's electric blue eyes went wide with shock.

'Coming, Ross?' Marnie's beautiful white skin

was full of bright colour, 'or would you like to go on eating?'

'Don't forget the mink, Marnie.' Drew McIvor was standing beside her, not wretched like the younger man, but somewhat amused.

'Thank you.' She tilted her head back to him as he slipped it around her shoulders. 'What time did you say Sunday?'

'How do you mean?' Liane exclaimed violently.

'What am I going to do with you, Marnie?' McIvor put her evening purse into her hand.

'It was you who suggested it, darling,' she retorted.

'Would you kindly tell me what's going on?' Liane said to Ross.

'Marnie's different,' Ross offered finally. 'I think she's just having a bit of fun.'

'Come on, Ross.' Marnie suddenly seized him by the arm. 'I have to be up early in the morning.'

'Are you always going to be a stable boy?' Liane asked sneeringly.

'I'm afraid so,' said Marnie. 'I can't pretend to be other than working class, not a ladylike, well-bred girl such as you.'

In the short, ensuing silence Ross sucked in his breath. 'Don't let any of us spoil our evening.'

'Let's go, then!' Marnie said, lifting her eyes to Drew McIvor as she spoke. 'You will give me a ring to confirm things, won't you?'

'Of course I will.' He smiled at her, sweet as honey. 'Whatever the differences between myself and your father, I don't see why we can't go on being friends.'

'What's all this about your friendship?' Ross asked dazedly when they were out in the car park.

'Just an impression I wanted to create.'

'Do you mean you wanted to take a rise out of Liane Maxwell?'

'Yes, I did,' said Marnie. 'She's a dear girl, but really too bitchy.'

'It was *you* who attacked her!' Ross said rather tactlessly.

'*Mea culpa*. Are you going to open the car?'

They had been driving ten minutes before Ross gave a bitter laugh. 'You know, it's funny, but for a minute back there at Ricco's, I was really jealous.'

'It doesn't sound to me as though you're over it.'

'The truth of it is, you and Drew seemed so intensely interested in each other,' he explained.

'How do you mean?' Marnie asked lightly.

'I've always liked and respected him so much. *Then*, I wanted to tell him to go to the devil. You're a beautiful girl, Marnie, and Drew's far from blind.'

'Don't worry,' Marnie pretended indifference. 'You misunderstood what you saw.'

'Maybe so,' Ross answered grudgingly, 'but Liane felt it too. She's in love with him. She's the right age for him and they have a whole lot in common.'

Before he let her out of the car, he pulled her to

him and kissed her grindingly. 'You're my girl, Marnie, and don't forget it!' His fingers on her delicate shoulders were hurting, and there was a surprisingly hard expression on his face.

'Are you quite through?' she asked icily. That was the way men saw women—*possessions!*

'Am I hurting you? I'm sorry.' Guiltily he released her. 'I don't think you realise how I feel about you, Marnie.'

'Obviously not,' she said, starting to feel worried. 'I like you very much, Ross, but I don't want to be serious.'

'Neither did I, but it's not working out that way.' Ross put his hand out and gently stroked her cheek. 'I've never met a girl who interested me so totally. You're terrific to look at and you respond to things so wonderfully. You're so alive, Marnie, so outgoing. I never dreamed I could talk to a girl like I talk to you. I think, when the time is right, I'd like to marry you.'

'Oh, *no*, Ross!' she cried, feeling worse by the minute. 'Marriage is such a big step and so far away. Why, you're not even through your studies.'

'I've got a good future, you know that. Next year, I move in with Dad.'

'Why, I've never even met your mother or your sisters,' Marnie said, flabbergasted.

'That can easily be arranged,' Ross told her a little doubtfully. 'Dad just happens to have told me if he were even ten years younger, he'd be mad about you himself.'

'Oh, Ross, let's just have fun!' she begged him.

'I'm not anywhere near ready for total commitment.'

'It wouldn't be so bad,' he smiled at her, then pressed a lingering kiss into her creamy neck. 'You smell so sweet, it's fantastic.'

She didn't answer, and because he was aroused, he thought her feelings were the same as his own. 'Marnie,' he muttered huskily, and sought her mouth again.

This time she submitted, trying to fathom why another kiss had fired her blood and this one didn't. Ross was groaning softly, covering her face with kisses, and though it wasn't at all unpleasant, she wasn't in the slightest danger of going up in flames.

'Let me hold you close, Marnie,' he whispered, stroking his fingers along the line of her throat. 'You're so beautiful, and I want you so much.'

His heartbeat was fast, too fast, but she wasn't ready. She liked Ross. She was really very fond of him but she didn't care enough for the intimacies he wanted. Some of her girl friends, she knew, did it all the time, but Marnie preferred not to.

'*Please*, Marnie,' Ross persisted, losing control by the minute.

'Well, *there* you are!' It was Tiny at the security gate, beaming his flashlight.

'Oh, God!' Ross groaned. 'Not right now!'

Frankly Marnie thought it was a beautiful piece of timing. None too coincidental either. Tiny was worse than her father.

'Thanks for tonight, Ross,' she said gently, and kissed his cheek. 'I'll walk up to the house. I'd like to.'

'That blasted Tiny is the perfect watchdog!' Ross said irritably. 'It's not the first time he's met us at the front gate.'

'True, but he's only checking,' Marnie said lightly. 'I'll see you Saturday, shall I?' She opened the door and turned her head back to look at him.

'Silver Lady's running,' he said. 'Not that she stands a chance against Drew's horse. You know he started like Dad, just a venture, now he's turning into another Sangster.' For the first time ever, there was a note of disgruntlement in his voice. 'You're surely not thinking of seeing him on your own?'

'Who do you want to come with me?' she replied. 'Goodnight, Ross. Drive carefully.'

Tiny shared her two-minute walk to the house.

'Did he say anything about McIvor changing stables?'

'You mean did he go along with our story?' It was chilly and Marnie clutched the mink around her shoulders.

'I've had a devil of a time from the Press,' Tiny growled. 'The only good thing is McIvor's keeping quiet. Another man could have talked plenty.'

'He owes Dad something,' Marnie said. 'Even if he truly believes Dad was fleecing him, he's had a tremendous amount of satisfaction out of our stable. There aren't all that many trainers as outstanding as Dad.'

'It was McIvor's horses that made our name,' Tiny pointed out fairly, throwing the beam of his torch from side to side. 'Not that I'm taking anything from Dave, but it makes one hell of a difference working quality. I remember the time. . . .'

Marnie listened as best she could, following a story she had heard a hundred times. Tiny's whole life had been horses, to such an extent that he had never apparently felt the need for a wife or a family or indeed any close human companionship. All the same, he was very loyal to her father and strangely protective of her.

'You have to decide on the spur of the moment,' Tiny was saying. 'I was a great little jockey in my day.'

'They lost a champ when they lost you,' Marnie encouraged him.

'Whatever made you play the fool with McIvor?' Tiny unexpectedly shot at her.

'What, this morning?' They had come to the base of the stairs and Marnie's hair gleamed brilliantly in the light.

'You don't want to antagonise him, Marnie,' Tiny lifted his peaked cap and scratched at a few bristling hairs. 'We're goin' to need his silence.'

'That's what I'm afraid of.' Marnie put out her hand and patted his arm. 'Thanks for walking me up to the house, Tiny. I'll come along with you in the morning.'

CHAPTER FOUR

THE horses were coming out for the big race of the day and stirs of excitement were rippling down the stands. Such moments were marvellous, and Marnie stood by the fence feeling the same thrill she always did at the sight of the beautiful animals she had loved all her life. It was impossible not to love them—the beauty, the speed and the courage, the dynamic power, and she felt the sting of tears at the back of her eyes.

Dalcarno was going by her, a brilliant but moody horse, and she nodded her head at Mick Carney, the strapper. The track was fast so Dalcarno had a good chance. In fact his trainer had unabashedly told reporters his big, handsome three-year-old was a past-the-post certainty. Of course Len Morris was inclined to rave about the classy members of his stable, but Dalcarno had a record to prove it.

'A penny for your thoughts?'

Marnie turned to see Ross smiling down at her.

'I was just wondering if Dalcarno had a chance.'

'He's got a lot of fanciers,' Ross looked after the tall, well-made racehorse, 'but I don't think he's going to beat Othello.'

Marnie glanced down at the racebook in her hand. 'I haven't seen McIvor, have you?'

'As a matter of fact I have. He'd just come from having a word with Othello's jockey. Further, I've heard it rùmoured he's negotiating to buy Gainsborough Lodge.'

'He's *what*?' Marnie's wandering gaze was jolted to a full stop. Gainsborough Lodge was one of the most successful studs in the country and certainly the most successful in the State. 'How would he find the time to breed horses? Or for that matter, why would he even want to?'

'It's just a rumour,' said Ross. 'He can leave it in the hands of a top class manager, but knowing Drew, he would have to become involved. He's one of those people who excel at anything they turn their attention to.'

'And what about the present owner?' Marnie returned her gaze to the horses.

'I understand he's thinking of giving up breeding. He was supposed to have had that heart attack, remember? Of course he has breeding interests in America as well.'

'Boy, isn't it nice to be a millionaire?' Marnie said dryly. 'I could tell him he'll never again find a better trainer than Dad.'

'What horse is that?' Ross asked her, getting off a difficult subject.

'Golden Slipper. I wouldn't overlook her either. The word is, she's at the top of her form.'

'Mother and the girls are here today,' Ross told her. 'Perhaps we could arrange for us all to meet later?'

'That would be nice.' Marnie lifted her binoculars and looked away along the fence with a show of concentration. She didn't really want to meet Ross's womenfolk at all. They seldom came to the races and only when one of their own horses was running and she had heard they were inclined to be 'very snobby'. Ross and his father were anything but, but she supposed it was too much to expect of the whole family.

'Actually I left them to come looking for you,' Ross told her, pleased that she was wearing a dress he approved of. 'We've brought a friend along, Melissa West. She went to school with the girls. We've known her for years. Her mother and mine are always rushing into one another's arms.'

'Sure they're not cooking up something for you?' Marnie couldn't resist saying it, mindful of what Drew McIvor had told her.

'No, of course not!' Ross frowned. 'Melissa is very pretty and sweet-natured, but she's not famous for her I.Q.'

'What *is* she famous for?' Marnie asked lightly. 'Seeing you're all such good friends.'

'Meet her and see for yourself,' Ross suggested, almost pleadingly. 'Mother is a bit stiff when you first meet her, but she's not at all like that really.'

'I understand,' said Marnie, and she did. Ross was trying to warn her.

The magnificent black Othello was first in to the starting gate and stood quietly. Her father had always said handled properly Othello would develop into the perfect racing machine, but his brilliance went hand in hand with a good deal of temperament. Now he stood pridefully, while lesser horses became fractious, handome head high and showing a decided look of his great sire, Black Magic.

'They're off!' Ross's attractive voice shook with excitement. 'Othello was the first away. God, isn't it terrific to watch him run?'

And it was. Othello loved racing, not accepting another horse in front of him. On his day, her father used to say, he could never be beaten.

Behind them in the stands, people were on their feet cheering. Othello was carrying the top weight and a lot of the punters' money and he was running strongly out in front, not apparently saving anything for the finish.

Another horse drew away from the ruck. Golden Slipper, carrying a top jockey who was all out to win, drew close to Othello's hip, stayed there and while her supporters yelled encouragement, she visibly dropped back. Othello was flying, revelling in the distance, losing nothing of his early, brilliant acceleration.

'God, where's his rival?' Ross was shouting.

Half way down the straight Dalcarno put on a surge of power, but his jockey had asked him too late. Othello stretched right out to his full potential, simply flew past the post with Dalcarno, flat out, a good two lengths behind him.

'You beauty!' Ross cried enthusiastically. 'Well, the shift didn't hurt him.'

Hurt by his tactlessness, Marnie swung away, and as she did so her eyes lifted automatically to the Members' Stand. There, in the centre of his entourage, was Drew McIvor, and draped ecstatically around his neck was Liane Maxwell, showing him and the world how thrilled she was that his horse had won.

'Won as he liked!' Ross was saying, but Marnie scarcely heard him. Why should she get such a jolting shock just because Drew McIvor was getting kissed by one of his girl-friends? What the hell! She was startled by her own rush of feeling. Let them all enjoy their victory. It was her father who had produced Othello a hundred per cent fit and McIvor had had the sense not to replace the jockey. Othello looked set now for a string of tearaway three-year-old wins.

It was quite a happy scene as the wife of the breeder led Othello back to the winners' circle followed by the smiling owner and his glamorous lady friend. Jack Wyatt, one of McIvor's new trainers, was hovering in the background, still none too sure if he was going to be able to work with his new client. For example, McIvor had insisted that Othello head the field the whole way despite the fact that Wyatt didn't like the plan at all. Anyway, the horse had won and McIvor's judgment was vindicated.

In the next race, Dave O'Connor had a runner and Marnie went around to see their horse saddled up.

'How I hate losing a champ.' Dave O'Connor's

thin features twisted in a wry grimace. 'He just
waltzed away, didn't he?'

'Forget it, Dad,' Marnie urged him.

'My goodness, I wish I could.' Dave turned
abruptly away from the bay filly and smiled ruefully at his daughter. 'Let's hope this one doesn't
run out of steam.'

It was exactly what the filly did, and for the time
being, at least, it seemed the O'Connor stable was
out of luck.

After the fifth, Marnie went off with Ross to
meet his family and stood with them while Silver
Lady ran a very dismal race indeed.

'In my opinion we should put her in other
hands,' Ross said angrily.

'The distance didn't really suit her,' Marnie
hunted up a tactful answer. It was quite understandable Ross was looking shattered. Silver Lady
was a full sister to the brilliant Silver Sovereign
and as a class horse wasn't living up to her pedi-
gree. Atlanta, who had always followed Marnie
around nudging her in the back, ran a magnificent
race, equalling the course record, and as Ross
observed gloomily: 'McIvor will have a job getting
all the loot home.'

Every time Marnie turned her head, she surprised one or other of Ross's womenfolk, includ-
ing Melissa, giving her a lynx-eyed inspection.

I must leave. I must go home, Marnie thought.
For the first time in her life the magic seemed to
have gone out of racing.

'Let's sit down and talk some more,' Mrs Drummond said. Somewhat mortified with Silver Lady's poor showing, she felt no actual sadness for the horse. Indeed she usually found race meetings a complete bore. 'What's the matter with you, Ross?' she chided him. 'You're drawing attention to yourself.'

'Sorry.' Ross lowered his tense body to the seat beside Marnie. 'Dad really should see Mr O'Connor. He's one of the best and he's available.'

'Quite,' said his mother dismissively. 'What beautiful hair you have, Marnie. So glossy and such a lovely colour.'

'There was a time I didn't like it at all,' Marnie answered her, smiling. Mrs Drummond was a handsome blonde woman, somewhat heavy in the figure and very zealously groomed, but Marnie found the coolness of her expression very off-putting.

The girls, sitting down on Mrs Drummond's other side, were still showering attention on Marnie's face and figure. Finally Melissa piped up. 'I've never met a lady jockey before.'

As Ross had already said, she wasn't any too bright, but she was delightful to look at.

'Marnie's not a jockey.' Ross stared fixedly at the girl as he spoke.

'Oh, you know what I mean!' Melissa gave a soft gurgle. 'Someone who rides for a living.'

'I love horses, that's all,' said Marnie.

'It's *not* all,' Ross answered sharply, angered by Melissa's silly sniggering. 'Marnie is a very accomplished rider. She's won many prizes for show-jumping.'

'Have you, my dear?' Mrs Drummond's thin eye-brows rose.

'It used to be my ambition to get into the Olympic team,' Marnie told them, 'but alas, I just haven't got the time.'

'You mean you're *that* good?' Ross's elder sister asked with the flicker of an unkind smile.

'Better than most,' Marnie answered evenly. But then of course it was true and her lifelong interest.

The other Drummond girl abandoned her inspection of Marnie's complexion to ask the question, 'It must be hard for you in a world full of men?'

'Why ever would you think that?' Marnie looked back into the supercilious, fair face. 'To begin with, don't most women prefer men?' And why ever not? Marnie thought wryly. Men didn't spend so much time trying to bring each other down.

Ross stood up abruptly, folding his race book. 'I think I'll have a few dollars on Show-off. Coming, Marnie?'

'You still haven't given me a winner,' Melissa complained.

'I'll give you one if you like,' Marnie made herself smile. 'Sure Tempo in the last. She's had seven wins out of twelve starts and she's never looked better.'

'Then I'll come with you.' Melissa got up gracefully and clutched at Ross's arm. 'I'll have to become accustomed to all this horseracing.'

There wouldn't be much point in asking why.

Melissa, Ross's sisters and most of all his mother, clearly had set plans.

In the betting ring she caught sight of Didi's blonde head and she excused herself hurriedly. Didi was looking up at Charlie Kingston, the bookie, putting a wad of notes into his hand.

'Oh, don't go!' Ross begged her in a tone of voice that made Melissa's pretty eyes narrow to slits.

'I must.' Marnie turned her head back to them. 'Nice to meet you, Melissa.'

'Did you see someone you know?' Melissa looked curiously around the swarming crowd.

'Yes,' Marnie smiled automatically. ' 'Bye now.'

When she tapped Didi on the shoulder, her step-mother nearly jumped out of her skin.

'How much was that you put on?' Marnie demanded, upset and uneasy.

'Just a few dollars,' Didi smiled brilliantly. 'I've had a run of bad luck, but that's going to change.'

'How much, Charlie?' Marnie edged around the stand.

'Just like she said, a few dollars.' Big redheaded Charlie looked faintly uncomfortable.

'Then why the blazes are your ears red?'

'Have a heart, Marnie,' Charlie grinned. 'Your stepma here doesn't back too many losers.'

It was pointless to say any more.

Didi took her arm engagingly. 'All right?'

'You know, Didi,' Marnie said seriously, 'I think you're well on the way towards becoming a compulsive gambler.'

'No, darlin',' Didi laughed. 'I'll never get to *that* stage!'

'I think you ought to tell me what was your last bet.'

'It's my own money!' Didi protested, a dazzling sparkle in her blue eyes. The betting far more than the racing visibly excited her.

'How much?'

'Two hundred,' Didi answered breezily. 'But honestly, darlin', this one is a dead cert.'

Two hundred! Marnie parted from her stepmother without another word. What she had said was true. Not some time in the future, but now— Didi was a compulsive gambler. Two hundred dollars far exceeded Didi's allowance for the week and probably took in some of the housekeeping money. Not that any of them starved; Didi was a superb cook.

Drew McIvor was standing talking to a friend, but when he caught sight of Marnie he came directly over to her.

'Marnie?' He took her arm, looking searchingly into her face.

'Oh, hello,' she responded tonelessly, unaware of all the curious eyes on them. Most people knew Drew McIvor, just as the racing fraternity knew Marnie was Dave O'Connor's daughter. 'Congratulations on a couple of great wins.'

'Smile, Marnie,' Drew told her quietly. 'There are a lot of heads turned in this direction.'

'I suppose we have to thank you for keeping silent.' She tilted her head to him, but for the life of her she couldn't raise the required smile.

'You look terribly unhappy.'

'Thanks to you!'

'You're blaming the wrong person, Marnie,' he said steadily, moving her along.

'You mean *you* are.'

'Did you come in your own car?' he asked her.

'Yes, I did.'

'Then I'll take you to it.'

All around them as they walked was the buzz of gossip. A young man who had had too much to drink lurched back against Marnie and Drew put out a hard hand and steadied him, his silver eyes frosty.

'Shorry,' the young man said, and gave Marnie a quick, cheeky grin.

'Won't dear Liane be needing you?' Marnie asked.

'Jealous?' He glanced down at her appraisingly.

'What else?' she quipped ironically. 'Really, I don't need you to walk me to my car.'

'I know what I'm doing, Marnie. For your sake we're going to stick to our story. Dave and I have had a private fight. It doesn't extend to you.'

'It's true, though, isn't it?' she challenged him. 'There's no love lost between us either.'

They had reached the car park and a cool breeze was blowing. 'I can't come with you tomorrow,' Marnie said jerkily, tossing her copper hair away from her face.

'Of course you will.' He took the key from her and unlocked her car.

'So you'll keep quiet?' she asked shakily. 'Is *that* it?'

'I guess.' He straightened up, his eyes narrowing
speculatively over her.

He was so sure of himself, she hated him.

'You've got fantastic eyes, Marnie,' he said, surprising her. 'Soft as a doe's and fierce as a spitting
kitten's.'

'I wish you'd stop playing games with me,' she
said aggressively.

'Really, Marnie,' the deep voice mocked her, 'I
don't go in for that sort of thing. Actually, my
friends have children, and as you're little more
than a child yourself, I thought you'd be a more
suitable companion.'

'Than Miss Maxwell?' He had opened the door
so she slid into the driving seat.

'Do you need to ask?' His eyes glittered at her,
startlingly light against the blackness of his brows
and lashes. 'Don't be afraid, Marnie. I only want
to help you.'

She trod on the accelerator so hard the little car
jerked forward in surprised protest. Her tension,
the need not to say too much or too little, was
telling on her. When she looked back in her rear
vision, she saw Drew McIvor's tall, immaculately
dressed figure. Even at a distance one could see the
sophistication and the infernal self-possession.

All the way home she calculated the risk of not
turning up in the morning, not because perversely
she wanted to, but with the determination that he
would get nothing whatever from her. On the
other hand, if he turned nasty, they could be in for
a lot of trouble. . . .

'I don't know. I just don't *know*!' Marnie muttered aloud. The idea that she was being manipulated for a purpose made her feel cold. Perhaps he wasn't really interested in Liane Maxwell at all. Or perhaps he had been, and wanted to get out of the situation. So engrossed was she in her thoughts, when the green light flashed she didn't respond.

A blaring horn shook her out of her speculations and she shifted off again, hardly hearing what the passenger in the passing car called out to her. No one had any manners on the road, least of all young men in panel vans!

Her father's expression when he came in was so much lighter Marnie looked at him in relieved surprise.

'Hi there!' Dave threw his hat so it came to rest neatly on its peg and went towards his daughter with both hands outstretched. 'Some good news anyway!'

'*Tell* me.' Marnie flung herself into her father's arms, feeling her heart lighten almost instantly.

'Jock Drummond is sending me Silver Lady and another two of his horses. Poor old Murph is in a bit of trouble. They think he'll be out for six months. The swab on Fleetwood showed traces of phenylbutazone.'

'Really?' Marnie stared up into her father's eyes. 'Is he going to appeal?'

'I'd say so, but if he's unsuccessful you know the rules, he'll have to transfer his team.'

'Silver Lady had a shocking run.'

'So she did.' Dave O'Connor patted his daughter's back. 'It has to be admitted Murph has lost his touch and in my opinion he's forgotten the golden rule: horses need the best, no matter what it costs. I'm fairly certain Murph was economising on feeding, and *that* you can't do.'

'So we've got three good horses, no less?'

'Not as good as we lost, but no matter. The thing that really hurts me is to be thought dishonest.'

They were speaking in near whispers now, in case Didi came in and heard them.

'No matter what he thinks, he didn't say anything,' Marnie said consolingly.

'That was preying on my mind,' Dave told her. 'I guess we owe him a lot.'

With their arms around each other, they walked into the living room. 'Would you like me to fix you a drink?' Marnie looked up at her father's thoughtful face.

'Just one.' Dave dropped into his favourite armchair. 'Didi won a lot of money.'

'She seems to be making a habit of it.' Marnie poured some whisky into a crystal tumbler and added a dash of soda.

'If you ask me,' Dave said with some anxiety, 'she's turning into a gambler.'

'Talk to her about it,' Marnie suggested, and put the glass into her father's hand.

'I don't think she feels it's got anything to do with me. It's her privilege to spend her own money.'

'If she only did that!' Marnie interrupted her father bleakly. 'If you don't realise now, Dad, that Didi is irresponsible, you never will.'

'Take it easy, darling, she might come in.' Dave wheeled his chair around to look towards the door.

'Where is she anyway?' Marnie demanded.

Dave closed his eyes and rubbed a hand across his freckled forehead. 'Unless I'm mistaken, she's gathering up some roses. We're having a celebration dinner at home. Thank God!'

'Mmmm,' Marnie had to smile. 'I'm almost sorry I'm going out.'

'Where to?' Dave took a sip more of his drink and sighed.

'The ballet. We're going in a crowd—the usual old gang.'

'Gosh, I'm tired!' Dave said in a faint voice. 'It's been one heck of a week, hasn't it?'

'And that's not all.' Marnie went to sit on the side of his armchair. 'Drew McIvor has asked me to go down the Coast tomorrow. He's visiting friends.'

'One moment,' Dave lifted his hand and brushed it before his eyes. 'What did you say?'

'You understood me correctly. The fact is, I'm as dumbfounded as you are.'

'And since when did McIvor take an interest in you?'

'Since he noticed she's no longer a child!' Didi told them from the door. She was clutching a dozen or more roses from the garden and she looked delightfully pretty and very much alive. 'Half your luck, Marnie. I *told* you.'

'Told her what?' Dave was looking angry and disturbed.

'She's so luscious the men will be clusterin' around her like bees to the honeypot. You should realise that, Davy. You can't keep your little girl for ever!'

'Can't I?' he thundered. 'Drew McIvor must be thirty-four or five. Marnie is eighteen!'

'Nineteen, Dad.' Marnie endeavoured to calm her father with a smile.

'Then frankly he's too old. And sophisticated as well. That's my view and I'm not going to change it.'

'Old fuddy-duddy,' Didi said chidingly, determined to embrace Marnie's cause. 'The trouble with you, Davy, is you resent all Marnie's admirers. I told you months ago Marnie was gettin' so attractive she'd be drawin' the men in droves. She can't be your perpetual little girl. You've always been a good father, but a mite strict.'

'Why think of that?' Dave said coldly. *'Strict!'*

'I won't go if you don't want me to,' Marnie said hurriedly. 'And strict is excessive. I'd call it caring.'

'Oh hell,' Didi laughed. 'Go if you want to. I'd simply jump at the chance myself, if I wasn't a happily married woman.'

'Dad?' Marnie looked at her father.

'Understand what I mean, I'm just puzzled why he's asked you. Everyone I encounter seems to think he's heading for the altar with that alarming Maxwell girl.'

'Why alarming?' Marnie asked.

'Oh, I detest women like that,' Dave said absently.

'Now *I'm* more your style!' Didi walked back into the room with a porcelain vase for the roses. 'What's wrong with Miss Maxwell is, she thinks she's just perfect.'

'Do you want to go, Marnie?' Dave asked.

She thought for a minute, afraid to say she was afraid not to. 'It's just possible I'll enjoy myself.'

'Then go,' Dave said quietly. 'He might be the big ladies' man, but don't fall in love with him. That would be the fatal error.'

'For goodness' sake, Davy!' Didi protested. 'They're only takin' a run down the Coast.'

'Maybe,' Dave shrugged his shoulders. 'But McIvor's scored with a lot of women. They love him, and it's not just for his money.'

'That's not going to happen to me, Dad,' Marnie paused in the doorway. 'Not at all.'

She didn't ride work in the morning and when she arrived at her front gate, Drew's silver Daimler was parked just outside. Its refined opulence did nothing to calm her, any more than the sight of him as he got out of the car.

'Good morning, Marnie.'

She looked up and saw mockery, sparkling challenge in his eyes. 'Indeed it is.'

'Shall we go?'

'And find out what this offer is all about?'

'Come on, Marnie, you want to.' He held the door open for her, seeing how her beautiful hair caught fire in the sun.

He was right, of course, and the colour leapt to her cheeks. She had never met anybody she responded to with such immediacy, and that in itself was a warning.

For most of the very pleasant journey they spoke about horses and racing identities, but never once did either of them mention Marnie's father; neither did Drew broach the subject of Gainsborough Lodge. His interests, she knew, were diversified, but he would have a lot to learn if he ever wanted to take over from Sloan Cameron.

'I hope your friends are expecting me?' She turned her head so she could see his handsome profile. He looked nonchalantly elegant in his casual gear, though there would have been nothing nonchalant about the price. Marnie had already noted the Gucci shoes and the 'Givenchy' stitched in white across the bottom of his soft dark green sweater.

'Of course they're expecting you, Marnie,' he told her reassuringly. 'In fact the children will probably pounce on you the moment we step out of the car.'

As a prediction, it was spot on.

'I know you,' the little boy announced, 'you're Marnie. Marnie, short for Margaret.'

'And you're?'

'I'm Christopher, that's Julie.'

With the two children clutching her hands, Marnie stood in the brilliant sunlight waiting for the smiling man and woman to reach her. The woman was lovely with a warm and generous face and the man couldn't have been anyone else but Christopher's father, the resemblance was so striking.

All of a sudden, Marnie felt very happy, and it showed in the wide tilt of her eyes and the way her mouth curled in an answering smile.

'Look out!' Christopher yelled suddenly, and as his mother turned her head, two excitable collies raced around the side of the house and charged the visitors.

'Who let them out?' their hostess cried, while Julie told Marnie sweetly that Glen, the male dog, was so intelligent he could open the garden gate himself.

Introductions were made in a welter of excited barking and though both dogs jumped up at Drew McIvor to be patted, Marnie noticed he wasn't the least concerned with protecting his clothes. He was obviously a dog-lover, and all the way up to the house, the dogs nudged him repeatedly for more attention.

'We've told them, Uncle Andrew, you'll take them to the beach.'

'And so I will!' Drew grabbed hold of five-year-old Julie and launched her on to his shoulder where she sat giggling delightedly.

'The children just love Drew,' Carol Brady told Marnie smilingly. 'I keep telling him he has to get

married and start a family of his own. He'll make
a wonderful father.'

'He's *my* godfather, you know,' Christopher
looked up at Marnie with his big dark eyes.
'Daddy and Uncle Andrew have been best friends
all their lives.'

'I love your house,' Marnie said sincerely.

'Daddy built it,' Christopher chatted away, his
hand still clutching Marnie's warmly. 'He's built
tons of houses around here.'

'Of course.' Only then did things click into
place. Brady Constructions were quality home
builders on the Coast.

The house was set up on a hillside with magnificent panoramic views of the ocean and the hin-
terland, and while Carol made the coffee and
Drew and Steven Brady stood talking, the children
insisted on showing Marnie all over the grounds.
The dogs came too, beautiful creatures, showing
magnificent winter coats. A large pool, surrounded
by timber decking and with a pergola half over,
dominated the rear of the house and both children
confided proudly that they had been swimming
'for years now' and they weren't in the least afraid
of deep water.

'Why haven't you got freckles?' Julie asked
gently. 'Susan Mellick in my class has hair like
yours, but she has a terrible problem with freckles.
She told me when she grows up she's going to have
them all off.'

'How silly,' said Christopher, and changed the
subject. 'Uncle Andrew told me you've won lots of

prizes for show-jumping. That must be thrilling! Have you ever fallen off?'

'I certainly have, and I've been handling horses all my life.' Marnie sat down on a redwood bench surrounded by soft plantings and the children sat down on either side of her, ready for the anecdotes that were to follow.

Afterwards, it was very hard to stop their questions, and Drew had to come looking for them.

'Coffee's made.' He smiled slowly at the peaceful scene; Marnie and the children with the dogs curled up at their feet.

'Oh, I'm sorry.' Instantly they all got up.

'Marnie has been telling us about the competitions she's been in,' Christopher said cheerfully. 'Have you ever seen her win a prize, Uncle Andrew?'

'Yes.'

'When?' Marnie looked at him with surprise.

'Last year at the Royal National. Not your first major win, but the first that I saw. Not only was your grooming superb, but I've never seen any young rider so cool and confident.'

'I had a top horse,' Marnie said sadly, still haunted by the loss of her beloved Plunder. All her best wins had been with Plunder. They had worked hard together all through the years— dressage, one-day events, three-day events, Plunder had been equal to all of them.

'Why don't you get yourself another good horse?' Drew suggested, aware that Plunder's courageous heart had given up on him.

'I couldn't, not just yet. Plunder and I grew up together. It's too soon.'

'And too soon for you to quit the ring,' he said gently. 'You're a wonderful rider, Marnie, and the greatest pleasure to watch.'

'I don't think anyone could take Plunder's place,' Marnie said loyally. 'He was a brilliant jumper and as game as they come.'

'Will you teach me?' Julie asked, her hand curled up inside Marnie's.

'I'd love to, darling,' Marnie smiled down into the flowerlike face, 'but I work all the time.'

'What do you do?'

'My father trains racehorses,' Marnie explained. 'He relies on me a lot.'

'D'you mean he trains Uncle Andrew's horses?' Christopher asked.

'He used to,' Marnie said, deciding on the truth.

Christopher stared up at her with his big dark eyes. 'What about now?'

He fired him, Marnie thought, but of course could not say. 'Now he's got someone else.'

'Oh.' Christopher looked confused. 'But he still likes *you?*'

'*Do* you?' Marnie asked Drew across the children's heads, one a dark blonde and the other a nut brown.

'How could you ask such a thing, Marnie?' The mockery sounded in his deep voice. 'Indeed it's hard to say which one I find the more beautiful, you or Julie.'

'Oh, *Marnie!*' the little girl exclaimed, her eyes

full of innocence and admiration. 'I haven't seen anything so pretty as red hair and no freckles.'

Christopher laughed so much he started coughing and they had to stop by the garden tap so he could have a drink of water. 'Why don't you tell Julie how rude she is?' he said finally.

Julie was about to protest, but Drew stopped her with a gesture. 'I know exactly what Julie means. One could write a sonnet extolling the whiteness of Marnie's skin.'

The day raced away after that, in the glorious winter sunshine. Marnie hadn't really expected the kind of warmth and kindness that was shown her and her initial sense of shyness quickly left her. The Bradys exuded an easy, entirely natural charm and the children were absolutely delightful.

They had lunch on the open-air terrace enjoying the sunshine and the wonderful view, and by the time it was over, Marnie felt she had been coming to the Bradys' for ever. Afterwards they piled into Steven's station wagon and found a deserted stretch of beach where the dogs could race madly herding the seagulls.

'What a perfect day!' Marnie, with her jeans rolled up, walked back from the water and sat down beside Carol.

'Isn't it!' Carol gave her attractive smile. 'It's been a great pleasure having you, Marnie. I'm so glad Drew brought you.'

'I still haven't figured out why,' Marnie confessed wryly. Carol had that special quality that invited confidences.

'*I* have.' Carol's answer was instantaneous. 'You're the direct opposite of Liane Maxwell. The last time Drew brought her, she ruined the whole day. She's one of those exotic hothouse flowers that doesn't go for kids and dogs and walks along the beach. Chris got excited and threw sand at her and she went absolutely crazy. What a folly! Drew didn't like it one bit.'

'But he likes *her*.'

'She's very attractive, I'll admit, and given the right setting can pour on the charm, but she's far from adaptable. Actually she quite upset me and I don't want her back. Not that I said anything of the kind to Drew, but I'm sure he realised.'

'Most people seem to think he's going to marry her,' observed Marnie.

'Oh, *no*!' Carol sounded dismayed. 'Steven and Drew have been close friends from the time they lived next door to each other as boys. I'd hate to see anything break up their friendship. Liane isn't the easiest person to take to. Neither Steven nor I have ever quite forgiven her—but then that's because we're doting parents. Chris was stunned. He'd never had anyone shout at him quite like that before. Actually the beach is no place for high fashion and it's impossible to avoid the sand.'

'Who would want to?' Marnie had her small, bare feet burrowed in. 'Well, for whatever reason, I'm glad I came. I've been searching for a little relaxation.'

'At your age, Marnie?' Carol looked closely at

the girl, amazed at the way she had fitted in so exactly.

'You're all so close,' Marnie said quietly, 'you must know Drew and my father broke up their partnership.'

'It must have taken a good deal.' Carol sat up, studying the play of lights on Marnie's hair and the flawless texture of her skin. 'They were so successful.'

'I can't bear seeing Dad hurt.'

'I can believe that, Marnie,' Carol said gently. 'You have a very tender heart.'

'Nothing makes any sense to me,' Marnie said, sifting the white sand through her fingers. 'I'm not really a friend of Drew's. Up until very recently he's always been Mr McIvor to me, a rich man in a rich man's world.'

'But you're attracted to him, Marnie. I can tell.'

'Really?' Marnie sighed. 'That's not the way it is. We're more like antagonists.'

'Not today.' Carol had to smile. 'You looked very happy together.'

'Now, Carol,' Marnie shook her head warningly, 'don't go making any schemes!'

'Well, it seems to me, you and Drew have a splendid rightness,' Carol insisted.

'My father doesn't think so,' said Marnie.

'Maybe he's hurting about something.'

'Oh, he is!' For an instant Marnie's velvety brown eyes looked pained.

'Things will work out, Marnie, and don't think because you're a lot younger than Drew you can't hold his attention. Drew has brought quite a few glamour girls down here, but none of them ever fitted in so easily, not with us and not with Drew. You're much more appealing than Liane Maxwell, in every way.'

Marnie smiled at her, knowing Carol was getting everything wrong. Drew McIvor had no serious interest in her, nor she in him. Attraction, and she had to admit it, was far from being everything. He had decided to bring her for the very reason Carol had given. He had known his friends would like her.

Julie was running towards them, her hair billowing in the sea breeze. 'Uncle Andrew said we must walk up to the lighthouse.'

'I know, I know.' Carol stirred herself, indolent as a cat in the golden sunlight.

'Help Mummy!' Julie cried, and between them, Marnie and the excited little girl pulled Carol to her feet.

'Daddy said we're going to ask you again,' Julie said, raising her shining eyes to Marnie's face.

'Great!' Marnie rested a hand on the child's silky head. 'I've loved being here.'

'I know.' Julie suddenly sagged against her. 'Chris is happy too.'

CHAPTER FIVE

In the car on the way home, Marnie stretched out luxuriously. 'I had a fantastic day. I really mean that.'

'They thought you were beautiful,' Drew told her.

'How incredible!'

'You think you're not?' His silver eyes slid over her, curled happily in the seat.

'Nothing special.' It was extraordinary how contented she was. 'I'd like a family like that,' she said dreamily. 'A boy and a girl. They're really the sweetest children, so sensitive and friendly.'

'What about a husband?' he asked casually.

'Does there have to be a husband?'

'Oh, definitely. Who else will look after the baby when you're riding work?'

'Depends on who it is,' she said seriously. 'I would want to give my whole time to my children if it were possible.'

'I was only kidding, Marnie. I'm sure you'll find the man who'll look after you completely.'

'Not Ross?' she asked slyly.

'Did you like Melissa?' he asked.

'I absolutely loved her. And his dear mamma and sisters.'

He laughed gently in his throat. 'Never mind. You'll be perfect for someone.'

'And who exactly are you waiting for?' she enquired sweetly.

'What would you say, Marnie, if I told you I'd found her?'

'I'd say you don't seem the type to let yourself be overwhelmed by passion. In which case, it has to be someone eminently suitable—attractive, witty, beautifully dressed, a little touch of hauteur. Someone like Liane Maxwell on her good days.'

'So Carol's been talking?'

Too late Marnie realised her slip. 'About Liane?' she lied easily. 'No.'

'I could see you with your heads together.'

'We weren't talking about you.'

'No?' He glanced at her with a sceptical smile. 'I know how Carol's mind works.'

'She's very fond of you,' she pointed out.

'And she doesn't want me to waste another year of my life without getting married. I'm used to it, naturally.'

'Well, I'm absolutely certain she wasn't considering me. At this point, we're little more than strangers with a serious rift between us.'

'Don't drag it out now, Marnie,' he drawled. 'It's been a very pleasant day.'

'And it's nearly over.'

'You can spend the rest of the evening with me.'

'Alone?'

'Quite alone.'

'I don't understand you at all,' she said shakily,

disconcerted by the tone of his voice. 'Haven't you got enough women in your life?'

'How do you figure that?'

'Good heavens, I've seen you with at least four!'

'And where was this?' He raised his black eyebrows.

'At the races.'

'My dear Marnie, I was only acting as their guide. Are you coming home with me or not?'

'I can't help getting the feeling you're using me in some ploy,' she said suspiciously.

'And so I am.' He reached for her hand and held it for a minute.

Something very frightening was happening inside of her, a feeling that was no good to anybody—least of all her.

She didn't remember much of their conversation for the rest of the journey, and Drew didn't even ask her again whether she was going home with him. Compulsion, not common sense, was uppermost, and Marnie wondered if she hadn't really fallen in love with him a long time ago.

When they arrived back at the house they found Liane Maxwell waiting, and she had been waiting for just on an hour.

'Drew!' The intensity of her voice as she rushed out into the entrance hall gave her feelings right away, the eagerness of her expression replaced by blinding shock. 'What on earth . . .?'

'Liane, this is a surprise!' Drew went forward suavely, though he didn't look especially glad to see her. Collins, the butler, was hovering uncertainly in the background almost wringing his hands, and Drew dismissed him with a nod.

It was as well he did, for Liane's vanity wasn't equal to the occasion. 'Am I going crazy?' she asked angrily. 'This is the second time I've seen you with this child!'

'Come along in, Marnie,' Drew turned back with slick urbanity. 'Liane can't make up her mind whose home she's in.'

Much as she disliked Liane, Marnie was kind enough not to want to witness her humiliation. 'Actually I'd prefer to miss this,' she muttered.

'It's got nothing to do with you, Marnie. Nothing.'

'Hasn't it now?' Liane challenged him bitterly. 'You've got a lot of explaining to do.'

'Don't be absurd!' His tone, though cool, was so cutting Marnie felt the actual lash of it on her skin.

'You'll be sorry, Miss O'Connor, if you interfere.' Liane's blue eyes were flashing and the colour had drained from the perfect oval of her face.

'Believe me, I don't want to,' Marnie said, and started to move back through the door.

'Marnie!' Drew got hold of her and stopped her before she had gone very far. 'I want you to stay.'

'So I can act as some kind of a buffer between you and your ex-love?'

'At the risk of not seeming a gentleman, I never ever told Liane I loved her. Believe me.'

'Then what's she carrying on for?' she asked dryly.

'I suppose one could call it the spoilt brat syndrome. Liane has gone a lifetime getting what she wants.'

'Perhaps you'd better call a cab,' Marnie suggested, shivering in the cool breeze.

'Come back inside, please, Marnie.' Impatience tightened his strong features. 'I suppose I'd better get it over all at once.'

It was obvious from Liane's expression that she never expected Marnie to return. In the past, a jealous rage had always been reliable, so she had concluded that Drew had sent Marnie on home. Now, at her reappearance, she felt a pang of terror, and it showed in the wildness of her expression.

'This is *your* doing!' she told Marnie jaggedly, clenching and unclenching her right hand.

'Do stop, Liane,' Drew faced her wearily. 'You're a very stylish lady. Act like one.'

'You're not going to make a fool out of me, Drew,' Liane said, so menacingly it made Marnie's skin crawl. 'I'm not someone you can put down and pick up again. You know everyone has been saying we're going to make a match of it.'

'I know,' he smiled sardonically. 'And I know who started it. I'm sorry, Liane. You're really very charming, but I don't like marriage proposals put in my mouth. Men are like that, you know.'

Liane gave a savage little laugh. 'You were happy enough with me until you began to notice this little bitch, with her father under a cloud. Why did you really take your horses away, Drew? Father is certain it was something O'Connor did, some kind of fraud. My father is a very astute man. I suppose it's on account of *her* you're covering for him.'

'You're talking nonsense!' Drew said tightly, catching Marnie's wrist.

'Am I?' Liane's blue eyes gleamed fanatically. 'It's been the talk of the racing world. I think it's about time I started asking a few questions myself.'

'Let's start with one,' Drew said curtly. 'What business is it of yours?'

'I'm neurotic,' Liane said slowly. 'Didn't you know?'

'It had dawned on me,' Drew retorted flatly. 'A pity, because you had a lot going for you.'

'*Drew!*' The finality in his tone got through to her and she flung herself at him with a moan.

'Have *you* got a problem!' Marnie's soft mouth twisted and she looked away from Drew with the sobbing woman in his arms and took the liberty of moving down the hallway to the library, where she knew there was a phone.

She slumped down into the chair behind the desk and put her head into her hands. What a dismal finish to a truly beautiful day! It was useless to pretend that little scene hadn't upset her, nor to escape the notion that she was being used. Drew McIvor was a heartless brute who treated women abominably. Even allowing for Liane Maxwell's unstable temperament it was certain he had made love to her and given her some reason to think she had a serious chance of becoming Mrs Drew McIvor.

Damn all men!

Marnie's nerves were in such a muddle she couldn't even remember the numbers for the local taxis. Where exactly did Drew keep the phone book, or for that matter the kind of thing they had at home—a telephone index?

She got up from the desk and as she did so she caught sight of herself in the huge gilded mirror that hung over the fireplace. She drew a little nearer, unnerved by her own appearance.

She was all eyes, and brilliant strands of hair across her cheeks. She looked quite different, glittery, and she stood frozen in place, staring at herself. Everything was moving too fast. A picture flashed across her brain of Drew McIvor talking to her father. Then he had been their major client, but a man far removed from their own world. He had always dazzled her with his looks and his wealth and that beautiful, mocking voice. Probably, despite the respectful coolness she had always accorded him, he had suspected her latent attraction. Now he was making her pay the price.

A car roared away and she visibly started. Had Drew taken Liane home? After all, she was Judge Maxwell's daughter, the pampered only daughter of an important man. What it was to have wealth, influence and a position in society! For the first time in her life Marnie seriously considered her general status.

Suddenly the library door opened and Drew stood there, making a Herculean effort to get a grip on his temper.

'I'm sorry, Marnie.'

'Well spoken,' she said dryly.

'Don't think I derive any pleasure from having women gloat over me,' he shrugged.

'Are you suggesting you're a sex symbol?'

'Millionaires are hard to come by.'

Obviously he was aroused, because his silver eyes slashed at her.

'That was pretty terrible, wasn't it, getting rid of her?' Marnie insisted.

'A damn sight harder than I first imagined.' He went to the cabinet and poured himself a neat Scotch. 'I thought I knew women, when in fact I know nothing.'

'You must be desolate!' She looked up at his tall figure, feeling like a puppet.

'Have you quite finished?' he drawled.

'No, not really,' her own quick temper was flaring out of control. 'You're a cold-blooded devil.'

'*Am* I?' The handsome face was formidable, a muscle moving along the taut jawline. 'Why don't we settle that, just for the record?'

So swift was his lunge for her, she hadn't the slightest chance of getting away. His mouth cut her breath off and because he found her so small, he lifted her off her feet and carried her to the huge chesterfield.

'It's impossible to teach you manners!' he muttered.

'And *you're* claiming them?' She wasn't going to surrender without a fight.

'Stop, Marnie. I don't want to hurt you.'

'You've done it already!' It was shocking really, a woman's puny strength. She was crying now, tears of rage, streaking down her flushed cheeks.

'No—don't. Don't cry.' He took her tears into his mouth and the sensuality of it nearly sent her over the edge. She gave a half smothered little moan, fighting with everything in her for emotional control.

'You're not crying about what Liane said?'

'Don't *talk* to me!' This was torture in its most exquisite form.

'It's not precisely what I had in mind,' he said softly.

'Don't.' She felt close to hysteria. 'Don't, don't, *don't*!'

'No use, Marnie,' he said tersely. 'You go out of your way to trigger me off.'

The extraordinary part of it was, she did. She heard herself make another strange little sound that carried its own precise message and he gathered her to him and crushed her mouth under his own.

The last time, his kiss had lasted seconds, now he seemed to have all the time in the world. He had released one of her hands and she placed it flat against his chest in a futile gesture.

'Open your mouth, Marnie.' His voice seemed shaken out of its normal calm.

She tried to resist, but he was teasing her lips with his own.

'Marnie?'

All resistance was turning to a panicky excitement, the feeling of being immersed in desire. His lovemaking was so skilful, the light caresses skimming, not coming to rest on her body, he must know she was ready to melt.

He put his mouth to her arched throat, then to the tender hollow, so that without her volition, her body pressed closer. Everything she had ever been taught seemed to be slipping away. She wanted him to kiss her again, only his mouth was wandering, her eyes, her cheeks, the lobes of her ears, increasing the tension.

Unable to stand it, she linked her hands behind his head, feeling the crisp resilience of his hair, silently demanding a greater satisfaction. When his mouth returned to hers, the pleasure was convulsive. This time she made no effort to keep her lips together and he kissed her so deeply, she felt frantic with elation, frustration, the monstrous quivering inside of her.

When his hand cupped her breast she went perfectly still, the blood rushing to her face because now he knew she wasn't wearing a bra. His fingers found the buttons on her little shaped vest, then her soft amethyst shirt, then his hand was moving over her bare skin.

She didn't think she could bear it; the pleasure was sheer agony.

'No!' She jerked wildly when his fingers teased the nipple.

Drew ignored her, lifting her slight body so that he could take the rosy nipple into his mouth.

'Please, Drew—*Andrew*, don't!'

At the fear in her voice, the youth and inexperience, he turned his head so it lay between her breasts.

'I'd never hurt you, Marnie,' he said huskily.

She was shaking with reaction, ripple on ripple of sensation spreading out from the very centre of her being. It was the most extraordinary thing in the whole world to be held captive in this man's arms, the two of them together, yet so fantastically right.

'Your heart's beating so quickly,' he said gently, pressing his head still closer to her body.

'You can't do this to me,' she whispered shakily, hungry for more of it.

'You're right.' He lifted his head, his eyes so brilliant they seemed to ray through her. 'When will you be twenty, for God's sake?'

'September. A few months.'

'I can still see the little girl in you.' His deep voice was spiked with wry humour.

'What do you want of me, Drew?' she asked humbly.

'*Andrew.*'

'Andrew,' she repeated after him, surprised by his insistence.

'I think I've scared you enough.' He was staring at her with an intense concentration, absorbed not only with the delicate bone structure but the brain that lay behind it. His eyes were narrowed, the bold black brows and lashes emphasising the startling light eyes—the concave planes of cheek and temple, the marked cleft in his chin. In short, he was beautiful as a man is beautiful, and at that moment his physical magnetism was unendurable.

'How many women have you slept with?' Marnie asked him, feeling her breath shorten at her own temerity.

'I'm thirty-four, Marnie.' His eyes opened now in anger.

'Your looks are against you. They drive women on.'

'Not *you*,' he said, with a bitter little smile. 'Can I be honest with you, Marnie? I've had any number of affairs and heaven knows Liane was briefly one of them, but I've never been guilty of deliberate cruelty in my life. Neither have I ever been able to say, I love you. Once or twice I thought it might happen, but it never did. I guess it's my nature—all or nothing.'

'And a speedy exit if necessary. I think the truth is, you simply want to walk away from involvement,' she accused him, convinced it was true.

As gently and expertly as he had undone buttons, he did them up again. 'You're way off there, Marnie.' His voice was very self-assured, rich in experience.

'I shouldn't have come back,' she murmured, evidently lost in remorse.

'You wanted to.'

'I wasn't entirely conscious of it at the time.'

He laughed and tilted her copper head right back, kissing her mouth.

She could, she supposed, have repulsed him, but such lovemaking was narcotic, leaving her body independent of her will.

'You're a fast learner,' Drew told her when he lifted his head.

'I'm concealing my true feelings.'

'You're worried, I think,' he said very gently. 'Don't get scared, Marnie. I'm taking you home.'

From fascination and the sometime flash of antagonism, she was hopelessly in love with him. She was obliged to accept it, because she constantly relived the time they had spent together to the minutest detail.

It's my age, she told herself condoningly, amazed she had travelled such a distance in a very short time. At nearly twenty, I'm all set for a violent affair. Proving, as it turned out, she was no exception to the rule.

There was no one to confide in, except the horses, and they were unsurpassable as listeners. Marnie had also taken to exclaiming aloud, explosive, traumatic gasps that one early morning training session made Silver Lady thresh about so wildly that Dave O'Connor rushed out on to the track, concerned to see the sweet-natured filly acting so unpredictably.

'What the devil are you doing, Marnie?'

'It's all right, Dad.' Marnie now had the thoroughbred quietened. 'I think she's a bit restive, wants to stretch her legs.'

'I can always rely on you for an answer.' Dave looked unconvinced. 'She doesn't usually get so excited.'

'I think it's encouraging,' Marnie stroked the filly's neck in apology. 'Why don't we ask her go give it all she's got?'

Dave thought for a moment, then jerked his finger at Tiny, up on Charleston. 'Marnie wants to give it a burst.'

'Ya can be sure of that!' Tiny snorted. It was hard to find a more high-spirited rider than Marnie. He considered the lovely, big filly for a few seconds, then gave his opinion. 'Well . . . she's lookin' well. Decent feed has given her a lot more energy and I think we're dead on with the trainin'. All right, Marnie,' he suddenly grinned maliciously, 'you're on!'

As a one-time top-liner, Tiny still hated to be beaten, but after all, it all came down to the horse.

'Come on, Lady,' Marnie bent low over the filly, whispering encouragement. 'Here's your chance to acquit yourself.'

'Don't think I'm gunna hold back,' Tiny cautioned her.

'Eat your heart out,' said Marnie, settling herself like an elf on the horse's back.

'Aye, you're a bonny little rider,' Tiny told her kindly, 'but a female.' If Tiny had a fault, he was the worst chauvinist in the world.

'You'll find out,' Marnie shot back compulsively. 'As a point of interest, females are among the finest riders in the world.'

'Not jockeys they ain't!' Seeing the occasional woman jockey always gave Tiny a terrible jolt. He would never get over it to the end of his days.

So engrossed were they in their continuing spate

of words, neither of them marked the arrival on the track of Jock Drummond, the filly's owner, and some little distance away, Drew McIvor together with his new trainer and Darryl Bell, one of the most masterful jockeys in the country.

But Dave had seen, and he felt a hot wave of shame and embarrassment and anger. He waved cheerfully at Jock Drummond and to avoid any possible confrontation with his ex-client moved out to give instructions to Marnie and Tiny, each trying to psyche the other out of a win.

'Drummond's here,' he said in a low voice.

'About time,' Tiny sniffed in the cool air.

'He *is* a working man,' Marnie pointed out fairly. 'Let's show him what his number one asset can do.'

'What's an asset?' asked Tiny, and looked at Marnie for the answer.

'Pass.' She was used to Tiny's sophisticated jokes.

'A little donkey.' Tiny sat in the saddle and choked with laughter.

Dave neither smiled nor relaxed. He waited patiently until Tiny had stopped shaking, then he told them quickly what he wanted them to do.

This morning Marnie felt super-confident, but there was no telling how she would have reacted had she known Drew McIvor was taking a vital interest in proceedings without giving that impression to his own trainer or the rather big-headed Darryl Bell.

There was none of the pressure of riding in a real race, but there was still the pleasure and the excitement. With a sprint, there was no hold-up early and gallop on home, it was speed all the way. They brought the horses around, both showing different styles and Tiny riding with a rod in his left leg, the legacy of a bad fall and the beginning of the end of his career, then they were away.

The wind was a song in Marnie's ears, the drumming of hooves on a fast track. ... Charleston had a big stride, but Silver Lady was impressively built for a filly and it was evident she had benefited from all the extra vitamins. They were racing neck and neck, Tiny looking determined and grim, but in the final hundred metres Silver Lady edged away and gloriously held on.

'Give it to 'em, girl!' Marnie was determined not to be collared on the line. 'Prove yourself worthy!'

And so she was! Even when Tiny put the pressure on, Charleston couldn't meet Silver Lady's gutsy effort.

'Good girl!' Marnie was stirred up and exhilarated, nursing the filly back to a trot. She expected Tiny to be swearing, saying insulting things about Charleston's breeding, but in fact he lifted his peaked cap and gave her the victory salute.

With the sudden release of tension, Marnie swayed a little in the saddle as she brought the horse back, even so a sixth sense—an instinct about horses—was working. At the very instant Silver Lady faltered, an icy chill ran down Marnie's spine, then with no further warning the filly slightly reared, staggered and fell like a stone to the track.

The way Marnie rolled clear showed her physical

and mental agility and a lifetime of coping with the unexpected in horses. When she jumped to her feet a little way off, she was quite uninjured, but certain in her mind that something was terribly wrong.

'Lady!' The filly was lying dead on the track and Marnie took one agonised look and burst into tears. Her immediate thought was that she had asked too much of her, never anticipating such a terrible result. She could never ever get used to seeing a horse die.

Her father was there and a score of other people, all talking excitedly at once. But Marnie's grief was intense. She hadn't changed very much from when she was a small girl facing the heart-break of losing her old piebald pony.

Jock Drummond, too, was taking it hard, but in a very different way from Marnie. He was glaring at his new trainer, as though there was a hoodoo on the whole stable.

'Glory be to God!' muttered Tiny in a stricken voice, and stepped back as a tall man walked hurriedly towards Marnie and held her arm. 'Not the first time I've seen a horse drop dead in its tracks.'

'That's no answer.' Jock Drummond stood up after his inspection of the dead horse. 'I'm glad to see you here, Drew. What do you think?'

'Only a veterinary surgeon will tell us.'

'You know how much that horse cost me?'

'It's insured, isn't it?' Dave asked tiredly. The shock was giving him those pains again around the heart.

'I'll want an autopsy,' said Drummond, looking

as though he suspected some criminal intent. 'I had the damnedest phone call last night.'

'What the hell is that supposed to mean?' Dave told himself to keep calm, but somehow he couldn't.

'Someone might possibly send for an official,' Drew McIvor said quietly, clearly to intervene.

'Already have,' an onlooker confirmed. He thought it likely owner and trainer might come to blows before then.

'Did you have to ride her so hard, Marnie?' Unreasonably Drummond turned on Marnie, the tears drying on her face.

'That's unlike you, Jock,' McIvor said flatly, while Dave O'Connor's face registered an angry disgust.

'Be that as it may,' Jock Drummond flushed, 'I had a pretty ugly phone call about my new trainer.'

'Saying what?' The bones stood out whitely on Dave's high, sharp cheekbones.

'I hardly know what!' Jock Drummond looked baffled and angry. 'For one thing, it was hardly more than a venomous whisper.'

'Then why didn't you hang up?' Marnie demanded, paying no attention to Drew's warning pressure on her shoulder.

'Not likely!' Jock Drummond gave her a look of open disapproval. 'Along with everybody else, I've never swallowed the story that was handed out to the press about Drew's break-up with the stable.'

'Yet you changed your own easy enough.' Tiny

emerged from his sorrowful world long enough to needle him.

'On McIvor's recommendation,' Jock Drummond returned belligerently. 'The phone call last night, that was upsetting enough to get me here—now *this*!'

'I'm sure the autopsy will show heart failure,' said Drew, regarding the older man with a mixture of sympathy and misgivings. 'I realise you've had a shock, Jock, but if you look around, you'll see so has everyone else.'

The area around them and the fallen Silver Lady was becoming crowded, but Drummond seemed to welcome an audience, hating the memory of that phone call, but still under its influence. 'Damn it all, Drew, let's get things out in the open. What about you and O'Connor? We've been friends for years, why are you holding things back?'

'They're coming to shift Silver Lady,' said Drew, suddenly remote. 'I'll take Marnie away.'

'Thank you.' Dave looked at his ex-client and nodded shortly.

'Hold it!' Jock Drummond threw out his hand in a driven gesture. 'My horse is dead and I want an answer.'

'You want the vet,' Tiny yelled suddenly. 'What are you tryin' to say anyway, Dave *killed* her?'

Drummond ignored him, looking straight at Drew McIvor. 'I want to know why you split with a man you once spoke of highly. What was it about him, his operation, you started to question?'

Drew swung around, tall and very formidable.

'Personal reasons, Jock.'

'Sure.' Drummond looked even more upset and angry. 'I suppose you admired his wife.'

Drew shrugged and pulled Marnie hard against his shoulder. 'The reason for our split, Jock, is right here.'

For an instant there was blank astonishment on Jock Drummond's face, then a series of expressions chased themselves across his ruddy countenance. *'Marnie?'* he asked in an embarrassed gulp.

'Don't be so bloody ridiculous!' Dave shouted.

'So that's it?' Everyone stared with Jock from Dave O'Connor to Drew McIvor with Marnie folded under his shoulder. Without the least suspicion, opinion had now settled on the kind of dispute that loomed in most families—an unsuitable romance. Without his even meaning to, Dave's outraged protest had lent credence to the charge. Drew McIvor was an experienced man, Marnie was still a teenager. Was it any wonder hostilities had arisen? People had been gossiping about McIvor for ages, as well they might do, with his millionaire friends and a string of girl-friends as sophisticated and experienced as himself. Marnie was only a little girl; most of them had seen her grow up.

'I just wonder if what I heard was sour grapes,' said Drummond. 'Could easily have been a woman, the voice was so odd.' Immediately he began to feel ashamed. After all, Drew was his *friend.*

Inside and out Marnie was cringing. Tenderhearted as a child, she was abnormally affected by the filly's sudden death. No one could have expected such a dreadful penalty for a brilliant turn of speed.

'What did I do?' she asked aloud.

'Hush, Marnie!' Drew looked down at her stricken face, knowing her grief was real.

'She just seemed to stagger.'

'I know.' Gently but firmly he kept her moving. He was shocked himself, recoiling from the death of a beautiful animal but toughened to a degree Marnie wasn't, or, he saw clearly, ever would be. For all her high spirits and quick tongue she was very sensitive and vulnerable, and for that reason he had to shelter her immediately from the sight of Silver Lady being lifted from the track.

When he put her in his car, she shut her eyes and told him she felt sick.

'Just shock.' He kept his voice quiet. 'Put your head down—that's it.'

After a minute she sat up, the nausea slipping away. 'What a loss,' she said bleakly. 'You don't think Mr Drummond could possibly blame Dad?'

'How *could* he?' She had slipped her hand into his and he held it tightly. 'The autopsy will disclose the cause of death. Probably heart. That was a brilliant effort and you handled her beautifully, but obviously there was some abnormality in the heart and lungs. No one could be blamed, Marnie. Racehorses are really very delicate creatures.'

'I *hate* it,' said Marnie, threatening to break down again. 'I've never ever had a horse. . . .'

'Don't distress yourself,' said Drew gently.

'That's easier said than done.' She felt incredibly shocked and miserable. 'She was looking so fit and well. Mr Drummond will probably blame Dad for his methods.'

'No, Marnie.' He stared directly down into her drowning eyes. 'Jock is a fair man. What really set him off was the phone call he spoke about.'

'Phone calls. *Phone calls!*' she cried wildly. 'Someone rang *you*, told you a pack of lies about Dad.'

'No lies,' he said quietly. 'I would never have accused your father, Marnie, without checking.'

'But it wasn't *Dad*. Oh God!' she could see he didn't believe her, didn't want to discuss it.

'I'll take you home,' he said.

'O.K.' She had never felt so depleted of energy.

'You didn't hear what I said to Jock, did you?' he asked, as they drove away from the track.

'Not really.' She had only heard what Jock Drummond had said to her father. How could he stand it, being so terribly misjudged?

'I thought not.' He glanced at her briefly. 'Someone is out to make trouble, you realise that?'

'You know what Dad says, it's a tough game.'

'And nothing to stop anyone saying anything they like over the telephone. I had to act and act fast. Put it down to my business training. I implied, Marnie, so pay attention, that you and I are romantically involved. Teenagers aren't usually my scene, but it was worth it to see the faces.'

She went to speak, but no sound came out.

'You look startled,' he drawled.

'I don't understand. . . .'

'I don't either.' Smoothly he overtook a car that had started to cling to the side of the road.

'And why would you say that?' Marnie pinched her arm hard as though to make certain this wasn't a nightmare.

'To allay suspicions,' he told her matter-of-factly. 'I'm certain I did. Jock's face was a study—undecided whether I was to be congratulated, or condemned. Your father helped with his little emotional outburst. Now everyone is convinced we fell out over you.'

'Good grief!' Marnie shook her head dumbly.

'Well, it was a decision, Marnie,' he told her. 'I'm not saying the right one, but it will be exciting to see how it all turns out.'

'I'm beginning to think you love manipulating people and situations,' she said crossly.

'Sometimes,' he said dryly, 'I have to. I'm presentable, Marnie. I've even been told I'm handsome.'

'I'll bet!' she muttered bitterly.

'I'm just giving you the facts,' he said, and turned his head.

He was handsome all right. Handsome and wicked and dangerous. She was even afraid of him.

'Your eyes, Marnie,' he said dryly. 'It's like looking into a mirror, very revealing. You don't fancy being romantically involved with me? As a sort of ploy to save your father?'

'Forget Dad,' she said sharply.

'We can't.' They were nearing the stables and he pulled into the driveway before the security gate. 'I mean, nothing will come of it. But *nothing*. We'll just see a good deal of each other until the end of the summer.'

'I'll let you know what I decide,' she said.

'No time to think, Marnie.' He stroked her cheek and she could feel her blood racing. 'We'll just have to make the best of it. Jock was even telling himself that phone call was sour grapes.'

'And so it was.'

'I'm sure it was,' he answered. 'Liane is a lousy actress.'

'Not Liane. Not *really*?' She was shocked.

'What a baby you are!' His shapely mouth was faintly indulgent. 'Didn't you realise Liane has a vindictive streak? A very jarring detail in so much grace.'

'People tend to get angry when you play games with them,' Marnie said.

'Underneath it all,' he said, 'little one, I'm kind.'

But *was* he? It took Marnie months, before she finally teased it all out.

CHAPTER SIX

NEWS travels fast on the grapevine and within a matter of days speculation on the McIvor/O'Connor split-up came to a halt. The affair that had smacked of 'fiddlin' and fraud' was now accepted as an affair of the heart. The inquest on Jock Drummond's fine sprinter, Silver Lady, revealed the nature of the calamity—heart attack—and Jock Drummond confided to the press that the filly had been well insured, but he didn't say for how much.

'All he thinks about is blasted investments,' Dave told his daughter in private. 'I don't think he gave a damn about the horse.' He shuddered at the memory of the fallen Silver Lady. 'I'm glad I'm having a week up North. It'll be good to get away.'

The following day he left with a string of horses for a Northern race meeting, and as Didi decided to go with him at the last moment, Marnie was left to a quiet house. Or so she thought. On the very first night, the phone rang continuously and each time she picked it up the caller waited for her hello, which subsequently grew sharper, then immediately hung up.

At first Marnie couldn't believe she was being

plagued by a nuisance caller. It seemed so moronic. After a while it didn't seem to matter that it
was moronic, it was so unpleasant. The only thing
to do was to ring Telecom. At least it was a free
call.

She hadn't even begun to dial the number,
before the phone rang again.

'Listen here,' she said furiously,' I've got the
boys from Telecom working on this call.'

'What!'

'Oh, it's you, Ross,' she said, for something to
say.

'I couldn't decide if I was on the right number,'
he told her.

'You haven't been trying to ring me before this?'
she asked him point blank.

'I've been simply bursting to, sweetie, but my
dad advised me to butt out.'

'Of what? What are you talking about?' she
asked irritably.

'You and McIvor, of course.' His voice sounded
frightfully jealous.

'He's not my husband,' Marnie pointed out,
obviously having reservations about telling the
truth.

'I say!' Ross gave a cracked laugh. 'He's starting
to influence you already.'

'Rubbish!' Marnie caught sight of her white face
in the mirror above the hall table. 'I think I have a
problem with a nuisance caller.'

'What's he saying?' Ross shrieked.

'Nothing, that's just it.'

'I'll be over.'

'Ross ... *Ross!*' Marnie was shaking her head vigorously, but Ross had already hung up.

When he arrived thirty minutes later, she had the phone off the hook.

'There are some queer fish around,' Ross said.

'More out than in.' Marnie stepped back to let him in the front door.

Disapproving as he was, Ross was nevertheless delighted to have been given an excuse to come round. He put a hand on Marnie's gleaming copper hair, his expression that of a lover. 'The next call I'll take,' he said firmly.

'I've taken the phone off the hook. I simply couldn't *stand* it.'

'Someone must know you're alone.'

'Millions,' said Marnie. 'Anyone who reads the Sports section.'

They walked into the living room, Marnie slumped into an armchair and Ross sat opposite her.

'Why don't you tell me everything?' he said, like a true lawyer.

'About what?' She lifted her almond eyes.

'It's simply not *you* to indulge in an illicit affair,' he explained.

'I beg your pardon?' Marnie began to feel alarmed it could have been Ross ringing her—irritating jealousy and so forth.

'I know McIvor might be devastating to a young girl,' Ross continued painfully, 'but there are deeper considerations. He's not the man to make you feel happy and secure.'

'I know that,' Marnie returned tartly, making Ross feel thoroughly mixed up.

'Then what's the attraction?' he asked helplessly.

'Sex, probably.'

'For God's sake!' He looked shocked.

'However, in my case it doesn't seem to matter. He has a superb sense of the fitness of things. A gentleman to the manner born.'

'Gentleman indeed!' Ross snorted. 'I seem to have met at least a dozen of his ex-mistresses.'

'That's unworthy of you, Ross,' she said heavily. 'I'm saddened to see you've turned on the man you once professed to admire.'

'That's before he pinched my girl.' Ross's right hand clenched into a fist, and his long, pleasant face looked unaccustomedly grim.

'Ghastly,' Marnie murmured, 'human emotions. Are you sure you weren't ringing me?' Ross looked up, displaying such hurt and incredulity that she immediately apologised, 'Sorry, but it had me pretty edgy.'

'Here,' Ross shifted over to her and knelt at her feet, 'let me comfort you.'

'And what would dear Melissa say?'

'Talk of Melissa won't put me off.' He put out his two hands and tightened them on her waist.

'Anyway,' Marnie said wryly, 'she's all yours. Just don't count on life being a bed of roses.'

'Never mind Melissa,' Ross leaned forward and kissed Marnie's throat. 'It's you I fancy—such a mixture!'

'Do you see me as the mother of your children?' she asked him, as much to put him off as anything else.

'What?' He lifted his head and gave her a fixed stare.

'You heard me.'

'Actually no,' he said, showing a remarkable lack of tact.

'So it's Melissa with her pretty, vapid face?'

'She'd just fit in, that's all,' Ross answered, goaded.

'Emptyheaded girl, with *your* mother to show all the better judgment—yes, I can quite see how she'd fit in.'

'Don't be bitchy.' Mournfully he searched her face, beautiful tilted eyes so soft and feminine, smooth creamy skin, tantalising mouth.

'Even as you're insulting me?' she snapped.

'I'm not. No, *never*!' He was genuinely startled.

'Then what *are* your intentions, seeing you're bent on questioning Drew McIvor's?'

'At least as honourable as his!'

'And who said *women* were bitches?' Marnie jeered.

'Well, that's the story. Good God, Marnie, whatever made you start on Melissa? I'd hoped you'd been missing me.'

'Well, I haven't!'

'You're in a wicked mood.' Ross sounded excited.

'On the contrary, I'm coming apart at the seams.'

'Oh, Marnie!' He stared at her curled up in the armchair. 'These are the best years of our lives, you know that?'

'No kidding!' Marnie groaned.

'I think I must love you,' Ross reached for her. 'I've never met a girl so completely bewitching!' Together they fell down on to the Flokati rug, Ross's fingers tangled in her hair. 'Don't stop me, Marnie, you're beautiful.'

'Is this real?' She lashed at him with her fist.

'My God, yes.' He had her pinned now, covering her face and neck with kisses.

He seemed tremendously heavy and strong, and just as Marnie was deciding what to do, like clobber him when she got the chance, the door bell rang.

Ross lifted his head tensely, fighting for composure, and Marnie got to her feet, her breathing as erratic as if she had raced up ten flights of stairs.

'Get up,' she hissed balefully, 'you look a perfect ass!'

'Who could it be?' Ross suddenly looked as if he wanted to disappear.

'Someone they know at the gate.' Marnie paused at the hall mirror to smooth her tumbled hair. She was wearing a canary-coloured sweater that seemed to accentuate the hectic flush in her cheeks and the extraordinary brilliance of her eyes.

'Well, well,' drawled Drew, when she finally opened the door.

'Has it started,' she asked tartly, 'our courtship?'

'I assure you when it does, you won't have other

gentleman callers.' Unsmilingly he went past her, seeing the little bruise that had started on her white neck.

'Ross is here,' she told him, thinking his eyes the iciest she had ever seen.

'Is that supposed to be news? His car is parked right outside.' His handsome face was expressionless, but looking closely Marnie could see he was far from pleased.

'Oh hi, Drew!' Ross had joined them in the hallway, almost knocking over the umbrella stand in his anxiety. Even to Marnie's eyes he looked the picture of guilt, his face all flushed and his thick hair mussed up.

Drew looked briefly at him, nodded, then turned back to Marnie. 'What's the matter with your phone? I've been trying for almost an hour to ring you, so I thought I'd drive over.'

'She's had a nuisance caller,' Ross informed him, obviously in a state of nerves.

'Have you?' The black brows drew together.

'Not a week goes by, but something happens,' Marnie returned flippantly to cover her own mounting anxieties.

'So you took it off the hook.' He didn't wait for an answer, but walked past her, found the phone and reconnected it. 'That was nice of you to come over, Ross.'

'Yes, I made a mad dash.' Ross decided to ignore the heavy sarcasm. 'Poor little thing was frightened.'

'Marnie?' He tilted a sceptical eyebrow.

'So there was Ross,' Marnie said, 'the flower of chivalry!' She was trying to inject some humour in what was developing into a tense situation. 'Now that we're all here, shall I make some coffee?'

'Do you have a drink on the premises?' Ross asked.

'Coke, orange juice. I have no idea where Dad hides the whisky.'

'Coffee will do.' Ross sighed and sat down again in an armchair. 'Who do you think it is, Drew?'

Drew didn't bother to answer, but turned to Marnie. 'Did you get on to Telecom?'

'I did.' She gave him a wide-eyed stare. 'One thing's certain, it's one of your friends.'

'You think so?' Unexpectedly his mouth quirked.

'What an odd thing for you to say!' Ross's voice was shocked. 'Ross's friends are all the very best people.'

'On *your* reckoning?' Marnie looked back at him sharply and just at that moment, the phone rang.

'I'll answer it.' Drew started away, while they both looked after him.

'You know what I think. . . .' Ross started, but Marnie hissed at him to be quiet.

'McIvor!' They heard his voice and Marnie realised for the first time she wouldn't care to cross him. Even Ross's eyes were as round as saucers.

The mystery caller hadn't rung off, because Drew was still talking, promising action.

'Did you hear *that*?' Ross looked inexplicably

frightened as though he were the guilty party. 'Whoever it is, he'll get them bounced into the clink.'

The receiver went down with a thud, then Drew came back into the living room, his eyes like frozen steel.

'I don't think you'll have any more problems.'

'I think you're right.' Ross loosened his tie. 'I've just remembered I have an early morning appointment, so I'll take myself off.'

'You're quite sure you won't have coffee?' Drew asked him politely.

'No, really!' Ross spoke briskly again, like a young lawyer. 'By the way, Marnie, it's Libbie's twenty-first at the end of the month. You'll be getting an invitation.'

'Will I?' Marnie would never have thought so herself, the Drummonds being what they were.

'You too, Drew. Of course.'

'Of course,' Marnie seconded insolently. 'A respected member of the community, which is to say, a rich man.'

'Well,' Ross smiled uncertainly, 'I'll take myself off.'

'Do you still want that coffee?' Marnie asked when she came back from seeing Ross off.

'Yes.' His voice sounded a little curt.

'Do you think it was dear Liane?' She rather hoped it was, and not some terrible man.

'I don't think you need to worry any more.'

'Whatever you say.' He looked so damned arrogant, inevitably Marnie's temper began to rise.

'Why do you encourage young Ross,' he asked tersely, 'sheer devilment?'

'A bit of that, I suppose,' she returned tartly. 'In any case, it's none of your business.'

'Words, Marnie,' he said shortly. 'Words to hide emotions.

'Don't you touch me!' She could hear her voice rising, high and scared.

'As if I have a mind to.' The note in his voice cut her nicely down to size. 'I just want you to think about what you're doing. Ross will marry his silly little Melissa and be reasonably happy. His father has even spoken to me about grooming him for a politician. Think what you'd be like, with your sharp tongue and forever trying to prove yourself a man's equal. Leave Ross and Melissa alone. They're two of a kind.'

'Gosh, I'd like to be big enough to throw you out!' she said heatedly.

'How you react!' He looked across at her, looking bored and cynical. 'Are you angry with me for interrupting a passionate little interlude?'

'Oh, shut up!' Marnie spun on her heel to make her escape to the kitchen, but he must have moved like a cougar pouncing on a kitten, for she was pulled back roughly into his arms and lifted completely off her feet.

'*Are* you?'

'Stop it!' The tears came to her eyes.

'I will when you stop fighting.' Drew let her slip down the length of his body, then he turned her around with his arms still locked around her slender body. 'I don't really like Ross kissing you, you know.'

'And how do you know he was?' Excitement gnawed away at her, desire that cut through her like a knife.

'Oh, Marnie.' His voice was both smouldering and dry. 'I think you both made that perfectly clear. Plus the little bruise on your neck.'

'That's the worst of white skin.' The entire time she was talking she was trembling and distracted, in a state of arousal, frightened to rest against him in case he felt the tremors right through her body.

'Right at this minute I'd like to see all of it.' His voice had a raspy edge to it, half erotic, half angry, and she had a crazy compulsion to start pulling off her clothes.

But of course she didn't, because she was naturally very modest and clung loyally to her own standards.

'You've gone very quiet,' he said, softly, and with a complete lack of his former terseness.

'I wish you'd go,' she whispered.

'I know that, Marnie,' he answered. 'And I know why. You're more frightened of yourself than you ever are of me.'

'I am *not*!'

'Then look at me.'

She lifted her head, her eyes big and velvety soft, and in answer he gathered her right into him and began to kiss her parted mouth.

There was none of Ross's frenzied haste, but a deep drowsy hunger that had every nerve in her

body jumping this way and that. She couldn't believe the way she felt, the extraordinary, unfulfilled
longings.

'*Please*, Andrew,' she begged him.

'Please, what?' His mouth broke away from her
own, to travel down her throat. 'Underneath,
Marnie, you're all fire.'

Her heart was beating so frantically, she felt
dizzy, less conscious now of her surroundings, the
fact that she didn't really know him at all. Phy-
sically he was perfect to her—the scent, the sound,
the sight of him, the exquisite mastery of his
mouth and hands.

'You want me to love you, don't you?' he said,
deep and quiet. 'Take you, Marnie, to my bed.'

His hand came under her soft sweater and he
began to stroke her back so she had to arch like a
cat with the pleasure. 'Little Marnie,' he said in a
whisper, and suddenly lifted her.

An image came to her mind of them both together, so shocking and convulsive she cried out in
a mixture of yearning and fright. This couldn't
happen, in her own home, however much she was
aching inside.

But Drew didn't carry her towards a bedroom at
all, but the kitchen, and she went mad all at once,
hitting him and crying.

'I know, darling,' he groaned, patiently waiting
until she had tired herself out. 'I know what it's
like to hurt inside.'

'You're just tormenting me, you know that?'
She could scarcely breathe with her little jerky
sobs.

'No matter how you feel now,' he said, suddenly holding her arms hard, 'you'd never forgive me later. I know you, Marnie. Everything goes deep, You're the kind of woman who wants to give your whole life to the one man. You're not at all sure about me, and I'm not going to hurt you. You've succeeded where nobody else has, in getting under my skin.'

'So isn't this all madness, our plan?'

'Depend on me not to lose control. I hope,' he added laconically. 'Let's have some coffee and sober up.'

Perhaps she flinched a little, because he leaned down and kissed her cheek. 'Have pity on me, baby. I'm trying to treat you as gently as I know how.'

To her surprise, she believed him. He had all kinds of disconcerting qualities. 'Physical attraction is the devil, isn't it?' she invited him to agree.

'You don't think we have more than that?'

'It's attraction, that's all.' She refused to answer.

'No one else makes me go to pieces.' He sounded as if he was humouring her. 'Put on the kettle, Marnie.'

'All right.' She drew away from him. 'It's stupid, animal magnetism.'

'It's been around a long time.' Drew swung out a chair and sat down, so male and immediate the kitchen seemed smaller than ever. 'What I really want to talk about is—I think I've found a horse you can bring up to the big time. A bold horse and a naturally big jumper, plenty of guts. He's done well in all the novice events and I think you'll find you'll have no bad habits to break.'

'What's his name?' She spun around in surprise.

'Salamander.'

'But I know that horse!' Her eyes widened in amazement. 'He's outstanding—or he will be in a few years' time. But surely he belongs to Jan Sutton?' She named a talented young show rider.

'It's commonly known she's prepared to sell.'

'She must be mad!' Marnie frowned, trying to think of a reason. 'That's a very promising horse and it must be quite valuable.'

'Since she's just got married, maybe she could do with the money.'

'How much are they asking?' Absently she spooned coffee into the percolator. 'It must be a lot for a class horse. Proven class.'

'That's not important at the moment.' Drew was watching her thoughtfully, still feeling the sweet taste of her mouth on his own. She had no idea of the depth of her responses, or what they did to a man. 'Why don't you come along with me and see the horse? Try it over a fence or two?'

'Oh, I couldn't,' she said ruefully. 'I'd never be able to afford it. Or the time. These days the standard is so high it's impossible to win without a lot of work. Apart from losing my dear Plunder, why do you think I discontinued riding? One has to put a lot of time and money into top class competition. Both were fairly limited until you took on Dad as your trainer. You made us, then you took it all away.'

'Don't be tedious, Marnie,' he said patiently. 'I did what I had to. Almost certainly your father will never try anything again. It's important, in my point of view, to learn this early. No one likes being ripped off. Dave'll make no mistake with Drummond and the others.'

'How dreadful that you won't believe me.' Marnie's voice was husky.

'Everything, but that.' He got up and switched on the outside lights. 'Before I leave I'm going to tell Kenny not to let anyone else in at any time. It's a mistake leaving you home by yourself. You obviously need a keeper.'

The following Saturday, Dave O'Connor had two wins and two placings at the North Queensland meeting, with Larry Sweeney, their apprentice jockey, riding brilliantly.

'You should have been here, love,' Dave rang his daughter. 'It gave me back a little heart.'

Didi too sounded thrilled and happy. 'I'd just love to stay here,' she enthused. 'The tropics are so romantic. It's like being on our second honeymoon.'

When she finally put down the phone, Marnie was still smiling. To her father, winning with his horses was the greatest thing in life, and Didi had a talent for making the best of everything. It was a pity really that they didn't have more time to relax together. Not that her father was actually capable of relaxing, being intense about everything and a naturally hard worker.

She wandered back into her bedroom with no compunction at all about borrowing one of Didi's dresses. Drew (she only called him Andrew in their unbridled moments) was taking her to a party and she simply had nothing really fashionable to wear except her tobacco silk, and he had already seen that. Nobody could deny his sartorial elegance, so it would be ridiculous not to try and match him. Mingling with his friends, so sophisticated in dress and mind, would put the finishing touch to their charade.

Already she could hear the whispers that would certainly go on behind her back.

Of course it can't last!

Where did you say he found her? Disparaging little sniggers.

But surely *Liane....*

We thought so!

Gossip, gossip, gossip; a lot of people were addicted to it, and especially about the rich.

She couldn't even count on Liane not being there. One couldn't expect her to go into hiding simply because she and McIvor were no longer on speaking terms.

By the time she was dressed, she was sick with nerves. It was easier to take a fence than a party, unless she was with her own friends. She wasn't so much concerned about what Drew's friends might think of her as what she might think of them. She had still not recovered from contact with Liane Maxwell. The thought of her was so unpleasant Marnie dismissed it from her mind.

At least Didi's dress was perfect—black chiffon splashed with brilliant flowers. With long fitting sleeves and a tiny waist, it could be fastened at the neck with the rouleau tie or left to plunge as low as one dared. Didi, who was very proud of her beautiful bosom, let her skin gleam almost to the waist, but when Marnie tried the same effect on herself she thought she looked very wicked indeed. So it was the tie at the neck and a little gold pin.

'You look beautiful, Marnie,' Drew told her. Of course he *would* say that. It was his function, paying extravagant compliments.

'I know,' she said kindly, trying to deflate him.

'By the way,' he said, without even pausing, 'Steven and Carol will be there. They're coming up from the Coast.'

'Oh, great!' Her brightened expression indicated her pleasure. 'How are the children?'

'Asking when I'm going to bring you down again.'

Marnie smiled, and when they were seated in the car asked a question. 'And what *is* this glorious occasion?'

'Wedding anniversary.'

'But I haven't got a present.' She swung her glowing head, glad she had gone to the trouble of having it salon blow-dried.

'Don't worry,' he said idly. 'I've got something from both of us.'

'Solid gold goblets?'

'They've only been married six months.'

'A long time these days.'

'I'm afraid marriage isn't as stable as it used to be,' he had to agree.

'I want mine to last for ever!' she said passionately.

'But of course, Marnie, it will.'

'Women can't take anything for granted any
more. Men don't seem to want them when they
lose their youth.'

'I can't bring myself to continue this discussion,
it's so mournful.'

'It's true.'

'Then you'd better marry someone a good deal
older than yourself,' he suggested, insouciant.

'Except that I want children, I don't think I
would marry at all.'

Her only response to that was a dry laugh.

The Nortons, his friends, had a beautiful home
in a hilly suburb with a superb night-time view. It
didn't have the romance or the expansive setting of
Drew's colonial mansion, but the contemporary
architecture and the beautifully lit landscaped
grounds were a triumph for the rather difficult
contour of the hillside.

'Robert's an architect,' Drew told her. 'I think
he's been very clever with what he's done here.'

Robert, in fact, greeted them at the door, his
lean, clever face beaming his pleasure. So
genuinely delighted did he look, he made Marnie
light up.

'Sally's in the kitchen,' he informed them with a
smile, his eyes dropping to the large, magnificently
wrapped box Drew was holding. 'I say, Drew, you
didn't have to do that!'

'I wanted to.'

'Thanks a lot.' Almost reverently their host took

charge of the gift. 'I'm quite dazzled, after our wedding present.'

'You don't know what it is yet,' Drew smiled.

'I know *you*.' Robert's blue eyes, behind his glasses, were full of a touching pleasure. 'Come on in, Marnie, and meet all our friends.'

Sally first, in the kitchen, a vivacious-looking long-stemmed brunette, brandishing a knife. 'Hi! Glad you're here.' Her smile was young and wide.

Robert kept them moving, introducing Marnie to everyone, and all Marnie could meet in anyone's eyes was friendship and pleasure. Carol and Steven were already there, Carol looking very dressed up and dishy, sporting her year-round tan.

'You look beautiful, Marnie,' she told the girl sincerely. 'I love your dress, it's exquisite!'

'It belongs to Didi,' Marnie leaned towards her and whispered, 'She takes dressing very seriously. She used to be a model.'

Carol laughed. 'Does she know you've got it?'

'No. She's up North with Dad, but she wouldn't mind. She's the easiest-going woman in the world.'

They sat there, laughing and talking away, and Drew and Steven came back to join them and afterwards an ever-changing circle of friends. It wasn't until after nine that someone called Laurinda arrived.

'Watch her,' Carol warned her. 'She's Liane Maxwell's dearest friend and a very acid young woman. I suspect the only reason she's here is because her husband is one of Robert's associates. A nice guy.' The expression on Carol's face was both humorous and rueful. 'Funny how nice, gentle men marry witches.'

When Marnie finally met Laurinda, instead of smiling, the other woman frowned. 'Oh, how do you do,' she said in a tight voice, 'I've been dying to meet you.'

What on earth for? Marnie thought, but didn't say.

'Can I get you a drink, Laurinda?' Steven intervened pleasantly.

'Lovely,' she said shortly. 'Brandy and dry.' Though she was very good-looking in a bone-thin, exotic way, her manner was so abrupt it was almost shocking.

Carol had been caught up half way across the room and she could see Drew helping behind the bar.

'Let's sit down,' said Laurinda, putting a claw-like hand on Marnie's arm. Her perfume was rather heavily musky and, despite herself, Marnie felt a thrill of repulsion.

'You know Liane is terribly agitated about the break-up with Drew?' Marnie did not reply and the older woman looked back at her sharply. 'I told her myself to let this little thing have its run.'

'What little thing?' Marnie raised her delicate darkened eyebrows.

'Don't be a fool,' said Laurinda, unimpressed. 'You can't possibly think *you* can hold him!' She eyed Marnie narrowly, trying to overlook the flawless skin, the glowing hair and the whole flowerlike appearance.

'That's life!' Marnie shrugged her shoulders philosophically, denying Laurinda the pleasure of hearing, why not?

'Drew has had scores of girls,' Laurinda gritted through her rather sharp white teeth.

'Am I supposed to hate him for it?'

'But never one like Liane.' Laurinda was discovering in herself the same animosity towards Marnie, her dear friend Liane had spoken about. 'If anything, they were perfect together.'

'I understood there were problems with her temperament.' Marnie looked towards Drew for help, but he had unaccountably disappeared.

'I think it's despicable what you've done,' said Laurinda with her surprising venom. 'Liane is brokenhearted—as well she might be. One of these days you might suffer yourself.'

'I'm suffering now,' Marnie said wryly. 'Do you always interfere in other people's affairs?'

'Liane is my dearest friend.'

'I'm sure she wouldn't want you to intercede on her behalf.'

'I'm sure she would!' Laurinda's jet black eyes flashed. 'By virtue of our long friendship. I can see at a glance what Drew sees in you. But believe me, dearie, it won't get you marriage. You may lie in his bed this very night, but he'll never take out a marriage licence. Not with you!'

'I'll bet your husband walks around with a splitting head,' Marnie said tartly. 'You're a mad woman.'

'Just look over there, girlie,' Laurinda hissed in

her ear. 'Our friend Drew can't resist a pretty woman.'

Drew had reappeared and he was indeed smiling down on a very glamorous-looking blonde in her early thirties.

'I mean, you're such a kid!' Laurinda breathed balefully. 'Drew likes older, sophisticated women, women who know the score, can meet him on his own ground.—Where are you going?'

Marnie had jumped up abruptly and the dark woman clutched at her arm.

'Anywhere away from you. This was a nice party until you arrived.'

'Guess what, darling,' Laurinda drawled. 'I'll be around at all the parties long after you're discarded and forgotten.'

'Crashing bores usually are!' Marnie flashed away, leaving the older woman with her mouth open.

Drew was still talking to the blonde, looking so amused and attentive Marnie allowed herself to be spirited away by Robert's youngest brother, who was still at university.

'Gosh, I never thought I'd get you to myself.' He drew her into a cosy little garden setting on the rear terrace. 'You're not really Drew's girl, are you?'

'Why do you say that?' Laurinda's spitting venom was having a delayed reaction and she felt shaky and robbed of all confidence. How could she be Drew's girl? A teenager and a virgin. She suddenly wanted to scream.

'Well, you're such a change from the usual. Better. Wonderful!' There was no mistaking the admiration. 'But so young and innocent.'

'Why should I be?' Marnie asked bitterly.

'I say, I haven't upset you?' Like his brother, Malcolm wore glasses and through them he peered at her uncertainly. 'I only mean you don't look in the least worldly like, say, his last girl-friend, Liane Maxwell.'

'Aren't men supposed to fancy innocent young girls?' Marnie asked bleakly. I'm only doing this for Dad, she told herself valiantly.

'They sure do!' Malcolm was forced to observe. 'I'm only jealous, that's all. Drew has it made—looks, style, a fantastic business brain. Even a string of winning horses. I understand your father was his ex-trainer.'

'Yes, they fought terribly about me.'

'I suppose your father will relent in the end?' Malcolm asked hopelessly.

'I've heard him say I'll marry Drew McIvor over his dead body.'

'As serious as that?' Malcolm, an inveterate talker, shook his head. 'Of course we all wondered what the split was about. Owners on a winning streak don't usually change stables.'

'Can't we talk of something else?' sighed Marnie.

'Better yet.' Malcolm lifted her to her feet. 'Let's dance.'

Some streak of recklessness, rebellion, got into Marnie, for thereafter she acted the life and soul of the party. Indulgent to her youth and enchanting appearance, people were very kind to her and she discovered in herself a real talent for acting.

But inside she was tormented, though still in a brilliant mood.

'Easy!' Drew came to her and pulled her gently into his arms.

'Oh, hello!' She gave him a tantalising, totally false smile.

'I need a couple of minutes of your company, surely?'

She had been dancing half the night, disco, dreamy, but not for a moment could she have forgotten herself in a man's arms. Until now.

'I've always thought you'd sparkle given the chance,' he said dryly, 'but I don't want you to burn yourself out.'

She could see the mocking smile that touched his mouth, the glinting silver eyes. How attractive he is, she thought dismally. So profoundly sexy. The need to get away from him was overwhelming.

'I think I'm tired!' She pulled away from him like a child who had stayed up too long.

'So we'll sit down.' He recaptured her hand.

'Let me *go*!' Now it was almost a tantrum. She was in a frenzy of desire.

'Don't think I won't carry you off and turn you over my knee,' he said very quietly and evenly, though she could feel his anger.

'I need a drink.' She put her hands to her flushed cheeks.

'Are you sure about that?' He was watching her without smiling.

'I've had very little so far.'

'How about a lime and soda?'

'Why not flavoured milk?' Marnie flung her head back and stared at him.

'You're angry with me about something.' His brilliant eyes narrowed. 'What's the matter?'

'Absolutely nothing. I'm having a wonderful time.' She looked away from him and plucked a camellia from a prolifically blossoming tree in a bronze planter. 'How's that, pink and red?' She thrust the perfect flower through her hair.

'I love it.'

'Don't try and fascinate me,' she said sternly.

'Stop worrying so much,' he said gently. 'You're safer with me than anyone else I know.'

Some elusive tenderness in his voice made her heart turn over. God, she wasn't only in love with him, he seemed to be all she wanted in life.

So tumultuous was the feeling, she spun away from him like a dryad and into the arms of probably the best dancer at the party, a very compact young man called Glen or Garry or something. He took her by the hand and led her step by step to the timber decking around the pool where a lot of people were dancing.

'What else can you do besides dance?' he asked her.

'Ride horses.'

'You, horsey?' He stared at her in amazement. 'I thought a true horsewoman looked sort of lean and brown and dreadfully plain.'

'I must admit there are a few of them about, but a lot more that look just like me.' Marnie said.

'And your pretty little feet!' Garry or Glen transferred his stare to her evening sandals, as though he had difficulty adjusting to the thought of her as a horsewoman. 'I suppose all that riding keeps you so lovely and slim.'

Marnie smiled at him but did not reply. How could Garry-Glen be a consolation? Never!

Just as she was feeling overheated and frayed a hand seemed to come out of the crowd and apply pressure to the middle of her back. It wasn't her partner, because he was a foot away from her, eyes closed, arms uplifted in the ecstasy of the dance, but then she had no more time to consider. Another tottering step and she overbalanced into the pool, going down in a rush of cold and shock, surfacing to see thirty or more startled and concerned faces.

'If you want to cool off, go ahead,' Drew bent down and said to her.

Across the grass, her hostess was running with a rug.

'She was pushed!' a woman said firmly, and even in her drenched state Marnie recognised Carol's angry voice.

With no regard whatever for his beautiful evening jacket, Drew helped Marnie out of the pool and steadied her.

'Here, dear, what a *shame*!' Sally put the rug around her and looked backwards at Carol as though to beg her to say no more.

'Of course these heels are absurd,' Marnie shivered, and her hostess cast on her a grateful glance.

'Come into the house, Marnie,' she said warmly,

'I've absolutely plenty of things for you to change into.'

In the master bedroom, while Marnie towelled herself off, Sally hunted up something suitable and Carol gave vent to her feelings of spite.

'I tell you, Sal, I *saw* her, and I saw the look on her face. I don't know what stopped me from pushing her in myself.'

'You couldn't be such a delinquent,' Sally muttered, upset that such a thing could happen to her guest—especially when another guest bore the blame. 'The only reason I asked her is because Tim works with Robert. I mean, he'd never go anywhere if we all banned him on account of his wife. She really is the most peculiar person, yet I believe she was brilliant at university.'

'Are you sure she just didn't write all the answers on her sleeve?' Carol said tartly. 'Poor little Marnie, she sure stirred up a hornets' nest when she captured Drew's heart.'

Marnie, coming out of the adjoining bathroom, caught the tail-end of what Carol was saying, but she couldn't possibly respond to it. Captured Drew McIvor's heart—what a laugh! Could there be a man more adroit at keeping his heart intact?

'Do you think the dress will come up all right if I have it dry-cleaned?' she asked the two women anxiously. 'It doesn't even belong to me.'

'Leave it to me,' said Sally with a competent air. 'The very least I can do.'

'The bitch!' Carol muttered again, looking as though she could choke.

'Forget it,' said Marnie, then immediately re-opened the subject. 'Did you *really* see her?'

'I did.' Carol's fine eyes sparkled. 'She looked exactly like the wicked witch in Snow White.'

'Poor old Tim!' Sally found herself saying. 'Do you suppose she's ever sweet to him?'

That set them laughing, and ten minutes later they all walked downstairs again just in time to witness a furious exchange of words between Laurinda and her usually meek and mild husband. The odd part was, quite a few of the guests didn't seem in the least averse to this form of entertainment. They stood around with varying degrees of encouragement on their faces, while Robert, as host, tried ineffectually to intervene.

'This is my party after all,' he said patently and carefully to two people who never even heard him.

His guests, on the other hand, were almost enjoying themselves except the few who hadn't quite forgotten their manners.

'I hope they don't start breaking things,' Sally said fearfully, plucking at her jersey sleeve.

His handsome face sardonic, Drew appeared at the back of them and took Marnie's arm. 'I think I'll take Marnie home, Sal,' he said quietly.

'A very good idea!' Carol observed. 'We were having such a lovely time.'

'I don't know what to say to you, Marnie.' Sally clutched Marnie's hand.

'Say you'll ask me again.' Marnie's wide mouth quirked in a smile.

'Home and safety!' said Drew when they were

cruising away in the car. 'I hope no one else gets hurt in the action.'

'How could anyone I don't know hate me?' Marnie asked helplessly. 'It must be socially very embarrassing to have a wife like that.'

'They say we get what we deserve,' he drawled cynically.

'But he's a nice man!' Inside the warm car she had stopped shivering.

'Too nice. Some women need a firm hand.'

'I wonder what's going to happen?' Marnie sighed shakily, and leaned back in the plush leather.

'Ring Sally in the morning and find out.'

'You don't seem to care!' she accused him, glancing at his dark profile.

'Oh, I care, Marnie,' he said dryly. 'I just have a different way of showing it. Attack can be met by attack, but in a less obvious way.'

'So what does that mean?' she asked sharply, disturbed by some note in his voice—a frightening ruthlessness, perhaps.

'At least you've stopped shivering,' he said, ignoring her question. 'Poor little Marnie, suffering for me.'

She closed her eyes and when she opened them again the car was drawing to a stop. 'This isn't home,' she said blankly.

'I've noticed your maidenly objection to being made love to on your own premises.' Drew pulled into his huge garage and turned the car off.

'I'm only your part-time girl-friend,' she said

heatedly. 'There's absolutely no need for this when we're on our own.'

'I know what I'm doing,' he smiled at her.

'No seduction scene.' She narrowed her eyes warningly.

'You're asking an awful lot, but all right, I agree.'

'Shake on it.'

Drew laughed beneath his breath, took her hand in his and carried it to his mouth.

The tremors started at once, the fatal attraction. She had heard so much about him. She had even seen him chatting a woman up with her own eyes. 'I don't trust you,' she whispered.

'That's my girl!'

Collins was still hovering, waiting for his employer to come home, but after he had made them coffee, he took himself off to his very comfortable and spacious quarters.

'Trust you to have a butler,' Marnie said reprovingly.

'Collins has worked for my family since he was fourteen years old. I assure you, comrade, he doesn't want to do anything else.'

'Was he ever given the chance?'

'Stop stirring, Marnie,' Drew said finally, 'and leave Collins alone.'

'I heard the other day you were thinking of buying into a breeding establishment. Is this true?'

'Not only true, but almost final.' He removed her coffee cup, then came to sit down beside her. 'Who told you?'

'I have my sources,' she said loftily. 'Who told you my dad was a crook?'

'Someone he should never trust again.'

'You mean he does?' Marnie was visibly agitated.

'Dave did very well today for Jock Drummond,' he sidetracked. 'A great pity he just didn't stick to training *my* horses. I'm not having anywhere near the same rapport with my other trainers.'

'I'm deeply unhappy for you,' she said sweetly.

'You don't give the impression of being happy at all.' She was wearing Sally's dress, a golden colour that suited her, but as it was two sizes bigger no matter how tightly she had belted it, it swam around her petite figure.

'You're to blame for a lot,' she burst out, then could have bitten her tongue.

'Don't worry, Marnie,' Drew said gently, 'something good will come out of the whole mess.'

'*God*,' she insisted, 'it was *you* who wanted it this way! Dad slaved his heart out working for you, twenty hours a day, seven days a week. I *told* you he wasn't responsible for the preparation of your bills. He left it all to Didi, though I told him plenty of times not to do it. So did Tiny. You ought to try Didi out on some calculations in her head,' she added. 'It's a pure freak, and so unexpected with her dolly look.'

'You don't feel any shame telling me this about your stepmother?' His silver eyes had grown cool.

'She's coming home tomorrow. I'm going to invite you over.'

'I'm not ready yet to speak to your father again. Don't forget I looked on him as a friend.'

Marnie jumped up in such a rage, she almost jerked the wrap-around dress off her. The silken cord that tied it at the waist fell free and she was wearing the minimum of Sally's underwear underneath. First the humiliation of being pushed in the pool, now this!

'You really should have picked out something to fit.' Drew picked up the silky gold and white cord and held it in his hands.

'It was the closest Sally had.'

'Take it off.'

She couldn't even seem to breathe properly. 'You know, I can't decide if you're Casanova or the Marquis de Sade.'

'Surely you're wearing a petticoat?' He sat staring up at her, fumbling with the dress. The light turned her hair into a brilliant halo around her small, determined face.

'What a night!' she sighed desperately. 'I suppose I'll be kidnapped next.'

'The truth is, little one, you already are.' Drew moved smoothly, pulling her back into his arms.

'Don't you know I can scream?' she asked him.

'I only want to kiss you. Every lady expects it.'

'You're a cruel, mocking devil!'

'That's right.' Deftly he had the dress off her, exposing Sally's satin and lace slip. 'We don't want to crush it.' Calmly he threw the dress into the opposite armchair, at the same time holding Marnie still in his lap.

'I'm not going to do *one* thing I don't want to,' she said, nearly distracted out of her mind.

'I won't ask you to.' He lifted her higher, cradling her like a child. 'Love me?' he asked simply.

'Of course I don't!'

'Liar.' He dropped a kiss on her shoulder. 'We're wild about each other.'

'For how long?'

'You'd be surprised.' His eyes had changed and for all his mocking manner she could feel the hunger in him.

His hand, that had been stroking her smooth skin, closed over her breast, burning through the satin. She couldn't help it, she let out a little shuddering gasp, at once unbearably aroused. 'You're my first real affair,' she said brokenly, 'it should never have been you.'

'Why not?' His silver eyes looked grave.

'Because you'll hurt me. You know you will. Desire is destructive if there's no love in it.'

'You can't feel any love in my hand?' He pushed the slip aside and caressed her naked breast.

It was too much. Marnie shut her eyes. 'Oh, *kiss* me,' she moaned.

The broken little request stirred him more tumultuously than she ever could have imagined. He crushed her body hard up against him and found her mouth, searching it so deeply the feeling of being completely taken over was tremendous. She didn't know it, but her hand had gone to his cheek, pressing down hard on the male-scented, raspy satin skin.

Her beautiful young breasts grew taut beneath his hands, her entire body burning.

'We've got to stop now, Marnie,' Drew said once.

But she had no idea why. This was so perfect, so ravishing, so fraught with deep feeling, she wanted him to keep on.

'God, I want you.' He bent her back, his silver eyes heavy-lidded and his face tense with passion. 'The more I get of you, the more I want.'

'Do you love me?'

'Yes,' he said grimly.

'Liar!'

It was the last answer she should have given, for he took her mouth again, violently, and she responded as though under all the passion they were indeed enemies.

It was a frenzy of emotion, a conflagration roaring out of control. Marnie made no sound at all, no plea to save herself, if that was what denying him meant. Her girlhood was over and she wanted this man desperately, wanted to know life at its most intense level.

When she did think to draw back, her voice failed her, her eyes blinded in a passion of tears and rapture. She knew that she loved him. Knew that her love had proved too strong.

The realisation of what he was doing made him ask her questions, but failed to stop him, his desperation seemingly as great as her own. He was shaking, and his voice so habitually smooth and controlled, broke on her name.

'*Marnie.*'

For an instant she had the wild hope that he loved her. All trace of violence had disappeared and the touch of his mouth and hands utter bliss.

'I love you,' she whispered.

'I know.' He kissed her, and it was so astonishingly tender she thought she would remember it for the rest of her life.

'I'll remember this,' she said dreamily, 'when I'm dying.'

'Oh, don't!' His voice sounded as shocked as though she were about to leave him.

He kissed her again, over and over until the storm of feeling could not be contained. There was the beating of a thousand wings in her ears.

Drew cried out her name. They clung to each other until she could feel him draw a tight breath as though to control the fire in them both. He moved slightly away and looking into her eyes said in a husky voice, 'Marnie, you must know I want you.' She didn't need to answer; she felt shooting excitement so high, it was like being transformed.

As she *was*.

She lay for a long while in his arms unable to speak and he cradled her gently, her lovely body relaxed within the curve of his arm.

The stars were out brilliantly when she finally got home, but the moon had sailed under a cloud. Drew loved her. She loved him. She couldn't bear to live otherwise.

CHAPTER SEVEN

A WEEK went by, when Marnie's feet hardly touched the ground. One late afternoon they went out to inspect Salamander, and as she took the horse over a few fences and ditches she thought she had never felt so happy in her life. Or indeed had expected to. Her knowledge of Drew's love, instead of unsettling her and causing her recriminations, had given her a sense of power and a great vigour for life. She felt wonderfully happy and secure like a blossoming inside.

It showed in her looks.

'You're in love with him, aren't you?' her father asked sadly.

'He's in love with *me*.'

'Don't make that mistake.' Unhappily Dave O'Connor looked into his daughter's shining eyes. 'If he harms you, I'll kill him.'

'Hush, Davey!' Didi put down her magazine, shocked. 'You're not a violent man.'

'Every man is when the time comes.' Dave stood up as though totally unsettled. 'You can tell him too that I won't allow him to buy you a valuable horse. I only wish I could buy it for you myself, but it will take a good while to get back to the position we were in before he removed the horses.'

'It's all my fault!' Didi suddenly wailed. 'How

much do you need?'

'He wants to buy it for me as a present.'

'Are you getting engaged, then?' Dave asked angrily, deeply disturbed at the turn of events. 'I think I'll have a word with McIvor.'

'Well, I think she's the luckiest girl in the world!' Didi jumped up and held Marnie's hand tightly. 'Why wouldn't *any* man love her? Happy she's a ravin' beauty and she has so much else to offer.'

'Let him fool around with his own kind,' Dave said grimly, equally jealous and afraid. 'Men like McIvor think they can do exactly as they please, but his money won't buy him protection. If he hurts Marnie, or causes her unhappiness, I'll break his neck.'

'But he's much bigger than you are,' Didi pointed out sensibly. 'You're usually such a loving father.'

'I *am* a loving father!' Dave shouted. 'And I'm determined to take care of my daughter, do you hear?'

'Sure do!' Didi retorted with an unaccustomed acid tone.

'I'm going down to the stables,' Dave announced. 'You can bet your life our Mr McIvor is going to hear from me tomorrow.'

'He's gone to Sydney, Dad.' Marnie ran after him, but he shook her away.

'He's too experienced for you, Marnie. Don't you know that?'

She said nothing in reply, but the first icy finger

of doubt touched her.

'Don't worry, darlin', your father will cool off. Fathers seem to make a habit of disapprovin' of their prospective son-in-laws.'

'He has never mentioned marriage,' Marnie said, gazing off into space.

'It doesn't pay to be too hasty, but I'm sure that's what he wants.' Didi got up, went to her handbag and extracted a roll of notes. 'Why don't you pop into town and buy yourself a new dress? I'd come with you, only Helen and Ray are coming for dinner.'

'But how much is here?' Marnie took the wad of what appeared to be fifties.

'Three hundred and fifty dollars,' Didi replied absently. 'Go to The Collection and let Jilly advise you. She'll know exactly what suits you.'

'But where did the money come from?' Marnie asked uncomfortably.

'Don't be silly, darlin', a big win.'

The Collection was possibly the most exclusive boutique in town showing the ultimate in day and night wear from all around the world. It was owned by a rich business man, but run by a woman of such absolute chic one completely forgot she had a quite ugly face. Her figure, however, was splendid for clothes, long and lean and almost bustless, and she had an infallible eye for what suited her and the customer.

When Marnie ventured into the large, beautifully appointed boutique, there were about six or seven elegant older women avidly examining the merchandise.

'What about this?' A blonde woman in perfect shape withdrew a dress from the rack and held it out for the black-clad manageress to inspect.

'No, darling,' Veronica said firmly. 'Sequins are not for you. If you take my advice, you'll try on the Jean Muir.'

'But such a price!'

'What is money when one wants to look divine?'

What indeed thought Marnie, thinking it was time to leave, but Veronica, for all her seeming indolence, had marked her for a sale.

'May I help you?' she asked in a tone of brisk friendliness.

'I'm looking for Jilly.'

Veronica looked puzzled. 'You must be Marnie?'

'I am.'

'Forgive me, the way Didi spoke I thought you were about ten years old.' Veronica grasped Marnie's arm and led her out of earshot. 'I haven't been called Jilly in years. Not since I used to run the modelling agency Didi worked for. Nowadays, Veronica suits me better.'

'I've never been in before,' Marnie ventured. 'Not at these prices.'

'You don't think I buy them here myself?' Veronica confided with a roll of eyes. 'I make 'em.'

'You must be very clever.' Marnie looked at the line and cut of the little black dress Veronica had on.

'I'd much rather have had your looks,' Veronica gave vent to a cry of frustration. 'Or Didi's. She was the prettiest girl on the books, but no sense at all. Not that I didn't like her and still do. It's impossible not to like Didi.'

'I agree,' said Marnie without confiding that Didi had almost cost them their living. 'She's given me some money to buy a dress.'

'Day, evening?' Veronica had already begun to sort out suitable things in her mind.

'Evening,' Marnie said without hesitation. It was the evening when she wanted to shine.

'Well, you've a perfect little figure—and that gorgeous colouring!'

Marnie couldn't remember how many dresses she tried on and they all looked good.

'Of course, we're scraping bottom with the money you've got,' added Veronica.

'It would feed a dozen families for a week.' All of a sudden Marnie felt guilty, without the proper values.

'In my day it would have fed us for a year!' Veronica had a clown's face, and Marnie burst out laughing.

'What about the cream and burnt apricot? It's the cheapest of the lot and I think it suits me.'

'Oh, it does!' Veronica seconded with infrequent genuine admiration. 'In fact I'm sure you've made the best choice.'

There was a slight commotion outside and Veronica frowned, looking suddenly like a dragon, then excused herself. 'Won't be a moment.'

When she came back she was still frowning. 'By our manners they shall know us!' She dropped her voice to a safe tone. 'They say it's a woman's nature to be bitchy, but honestly, the types I get in here! Some of them even forget the staff are human beings.'

Veronica led the way out with the new dress and the money, and Marnie followed. It was amazing what a dress did. Amazing how beautiful she wanted to look for the man she loved.

Buoyant with dreams, she nodded pleasantly at an older woman who returned her little half smile, but as she walked to the counter the afternoon's adventure came to a halt. Laurinda Vaughn was staring at her with an urgent intensity, like the devil waiting on a soul.

Marnie felt stifled, but realised she didn't have any choice but to continue walking to the counter.

'Why, look who's here!' Laurinda called in a voice that would have been beautiful but for the inbuilt sneer.

'You know one another?' Veronica, lovingly folding the model dress into tissue paper, looked up surprised. Laurinda Vaughn was one of her best customers, but about as lovable as a cobra.

'Slightly.' For the life of her Marnie couldn't pretend friendliness.

'And what have you got there?' Rudely Laurinda reached over and pulled back the tissue paper folds. 'A little present, I'm sure.'

'Yes, from my stepmother.'

'It's lovely.' Laurinda gave her Borgia smile. 'I hear Drew's in Sydney?'

'Yes.' Marnie was grateful to Veronica, who was

clearly hurrying.

'Liane told me when she rang last night. They're staying at the Boulevard, aren't they?'

'There you are, my dear!' Veronica said bracingly, seeing the girl had lost all her bright colour. 'I'm free to attend to you now, Mrs Vaughn.' More's the pity, she thought fastidiously. An odd woman, such an odd woman, but she couldn't make out why Marnie had gone so white.

'Remember what I told you?' Seemingly bored, Laurinda prepared to move on. 'It looks rather as if they're back together, wouldn't you say?'

Don't believe it, Marnie told herself. Don't let her tarnish you with her jealousy and spite.

All that night long she tossed and turned. It would have been easier to have rung the Boulevard and made sure, but such an action had gone completely against the grain. She loathed the idea of checking on Drew. Even Liane. Love was nothing without trust.

Next morning she did some fast work with Tiny at the track, but by the time she got home she had a violent headache.

'What's the matter?' Didi peered at her anxiously. 'It's not like you to have a headache, much less lie down.'

'I'm sorry,' said Marnie.

'Never mind that.' Didi sat down on the bed and took Marnie's hand. 'There's something botherin' you, isn't there? One minute you were on top of the world, now this.'

'Do you really think it's possible Drew loves

me?' asked Marnie urgently.

'Honey, every woman has her moment of doubt. I guess it's because love is so important to us. He's a busy man. Don't fret because he hasn't rung. You know the position with your father. Drew mightn't like to ring here.'

'It's not *that* I'm worrying about.' Marnie turned her face towards the window. 'I've slept with him, Dee.'

'You've *what*?' Didi looked as if she was about to pass out.

'It just happened. One wonders how, in the cold light of day.'

'So now you're wonderin'. . . .' Didi looked as if she was about to cry.

'No.' Marnie shook her head. 'Not that. I met a friend of Liane Maxwell's today, and she told me they were together in Sydney. She even knew the name of his hotel.'

'I don't believe it!' Didi exclaimed furiously.

'How would she know the hotel?'

'I don't care.' Didi was stirred to unaccustomed wrath.

Marnie shook her head wonderingly, as if trying to understand herself. 'I don't regret loving him, Dee.'

'Then why are your eyes filled with tears?'

'I thought he loved me,' explained Marnie.

'Some men need women,' Didi sighed, 'but I can't say I thought it applied to Drew McIvor. He's an amazingly attractive man, but he's never struck me as a womaniser. To be fair to him, it's the women who chase him. Why don't we just call the Boulevard and make sure?'

'Act the spy?' Marnie said bitterly.

'Why not? It's better than puttin' yourself through this torture. If he's there with Miss Maxwell you can cut your losses and move on.'

'Oh, God, Dee!' Marnie buried her head babylike in the pillows. 'I couldn't bear it.'

'We all go through heartbreak,' Didi spoke from experience. 'Why, I was once in a predicament myself.'

'Oh, *help* me!' Marnie moaned. Her one perfect love had exposed her to bitter pain.

'Just you lie there, honey,' Didi patted her with a maternal hand. 'I'm goin' to do a little checking.'

At that, Marnie swung over on her back, but she didn't move. 'It seems so sordid, Dee,' she sighed.

'That's life!'

Didi escaped before Marnie stopped her and after a minute Marnie jumped up. She had to be there when Didi rang.

'Thank you,' Didi was saying. 'They're connectin' me to Miss Maxwell's room.'

'So she's there.' Marnie came down heavily in a chair.

'Still ringin',' said Didi.

'Hang up.' Marnie's young face had sterned so that she indeed did look like her paternal grandmother. 'I don't want to go on with this any more.'

Didi gave a great quiescent sigh but waited until

the hotel receptionist told her Miss Maxwell wasn't answering.

'Thank you,' she said without her pretty Southern drawl, and hung up.

'So she joined him,' said Marnie.

'Don't abandon hope,' urged Didi.

'I think I *have* to,' Marnie said quietly, her face as cold as alabaster. 'He does care for me in his way, but he expects to do exactly as he likes.'

'Don't they all!' Didi said without complaint. 'Surely you're not goin' to give him up without a fight?'

'I don't know *how* I feel,' said Marnie. 'Maybe numb. If a woman gives herself, she feels that's it! I'm giving you everything I am, heart and body and soul. I'm afraid men don't think like that. Worse, they've filled our heads with all their notions to keep us firmly in our place.'

'Times have changed, Marnie,' Didi told her. 'Look at your friend Jo-Ann livin' with her boy-friend. I'm not sure if it isn't the better way. There were plenty of terrible shocks in the old days.'

'But of course a lot of people think it's cheap,' Marnie said mournfully. 'Not for Mark, but for Jo-Ann. The age-old story, a man can do as he likes, but a woman is supposed to spend her entire life guarding her honour.'

'Where did we go wrong?' sighed Didi.

When Drew returned, he had a very special present for Marnie.

'You've lost weight,' he told her, his brilliant

eyes savouring the fragile picture she made.

'I missed you,' she said with the sweetest smile.

'And I you!' He drew her into his arms and kissed her deeply. 'I never ever expected to find anyone like you.'

It was a stupendous effort to fight out of her swirling senses, but Marnie was discovering she had a steely core. She wasn't such a fool she didn't know she had certain assets that could keep him at her side. In fact their affair might turn out not quite as he expected. Who knows he might even be made to suffer a little pain himself.

'How was the trip?' she asked him as he delved in his breast pocket.

'Very quiet.'

Lie away, she thought. 'Didn't see anyone you know?' She tilted her head back in delicious idleness to make the question seem even more casual.

'Only business acquaintances,' he dismissed the trip lightly. 'Give me your finger.'

She sat very still. 'A friendship ring?'

'Friendship you may be sure.' He took her unresistant hand. 'I'm not boring you, am I?'

She turned swiftly at that, fighting back into her role. 'I'm always flippant when I'm hurting. You were away so long.'

His eyes narrowed very slightly, but he slipped the exquisite ruby and diamond ring on the third finger of her left hand. 'I wanted colour in the stone. Something glowing—like you. Well?' he asked, when she didn't speak.

'Perhaps I need a bit more time.'

'I daresay you do,' he spoke dryly, 'but I'm more conscious of the passing years. I want you, Marnie, and I want you now!'

'Why me?' She made her voice very small and humble.

'You're the most entertaining girl in the world.'

So they were engaged.

I'll make him fall hopelessly in love with me, Marnie swore to herself. I'll work at it as hard as I know how, without surrendering this body he craves.

Strangely enough, Drew didn't ask her, as though he too was playing a game. Run along, he said, on the evenings they went out.

Run along? It was far from lover-like.

'If this were the movies,' Marnie told Didi, 'I'd hire a private investigator to watch his every movement. Then we'd have the big scene where I throw his ring in his face and stalk away.'

'With the private investigator,' Didi laughed merrily.

Her father was very quiet as though he couldn't quite believe it all, but his anger seemed gone. Drew had spoken to him privately, and though Dave's smiles didn't come easily to him, he seemed prepared to take each day calmly.

'We're hotblooded people, I suppose,' he said to Marnie. 'I never thought I'd lose you so early.'

'Nonsense!' Marnie protested, almost giving the game away.

Now that she was so neatly disposed of, the Drummond women were intent on being friendly, each having rung her one by one.

'I expect you and Drew will be giving a big party?' Mrs Drummond drooled, somewhat mystified when Marnie replied that she preferred a quiet, private celebration.

She mentioned this to Drew when they were driving down the Coast one Sunday to see Carol and Steven.

'Do you want one?' he asked.

'On second thoughts,' she said, 'I do. Let's ask all your old girl-friends.'

If she was hoping he'd confide in her, he didn't. 'You should wear yellow more often,' he said. 'It's very becoming.'

When they arrived Marnie was hugged and kissed by all. So happy did they all seem, it distressed Marnie to think she was purposely misleading her friends.

'We had such a dreadful time thinking it might have been Liane Maxwell, the relief and pleasure is overwhelming,' Carol confided. 'I know you'll both be very, very happy.'

So what, thought Marnie, can I reply? That it *was* Liane Maxwell and forever will be when he wants her? It took a great deal for her to hold her tongue.

After lunch they sat on the glorious beach watching the ocean pound in.

'I think I'll have a swim,' Marnie announced.

'In what?' Drew raised his eyebrow.

'I have my togs on underneath.' As indeed she had.

The children laughed excitedly and jumped up and down. 'Can we too, Mummy?'

Without the least selfconsciousness Marnie stripped off her shirt and jeans, and Carol decided the children could go in in their shorts.

'Don't go out, Marnie,' Drew warned her, while Steven got to his feet to watch the children. 'This is an unpatrolled beach.'

'I'll take care.'

The water was still rather cold, but the sun was shining brilliantly. It was a heavenly day, typical Queensland winter weather.

In the foaming shallows the children shrieked their delight, but Marnie, a good swimmer, walked out to catch a breaker.

Glorious! She dived under a turquoise wave and surfaced, slicking back her wet hair.

Carol and Drew clapped from the beach and Steven lamented that he hadn't brought his camera.

Like a mermaid she sported for perhaps fifteen minutes, then she started to get cold. One more wave, then she'd go in.

When the rip caught her, at first she didn't panic. She knew exactly what to do. She swam with it for a while, then tried to cut across on the diagonal, but it was proving too strong.

On the beach Carol went to grasp Drew's arm, but he was already on his feet. 'God help me, she's in trouble!'

Steven had his back to the whole drama, watching the children surfing in on the glistening waves.

She was being carried farther along the beach.

So this is how it happens, she thought. We think we're immortal, then it's all over. There wasn't one cloud in the whole perfect sky, the balmy breeze still blew and the surf tumbled in forever.

She wasn't even fighting as she should. Never to have out of life what she really wanted—oh, Drew!

He saw her face as he threshed closer and he was terribly afraid.

'Hold on, Marnie, I'm coming!'

Normally a powerful swimmer, he now cut through the water like a shark.

Her strange apathy had only lasted for a moment, then the lust for life whipped back through her body. He reached her and got her in tow, fearless of his own life, kicking out strongly disregarding the hindrance of his clothes.

On the beach they were all standing, sick with dread. The children were crying, Julie with her eyes screwed tight. Steven had gone to their assistance, but now it was obvious Drew had brought them both out of the rip.

'Thank God!' Carol's knees buckled under her and she sat down heavily on the beach. 'Look, children, it's all right. See Uncle Drew? Julie, open your eyes.'

Christopher tightened his grip around his mother's neck. 'I'm not ever going to swim anywhere but between the flags.'

On the way home he was so silent and remote, he might just as well have been alone.

'Why didn't you just let me go?' she said tearfully, upset by his attitude.

'How *dare* you!' He swung the car off the high-way and pulled up. 'What's this all about, Marnie?'

'I don't understand you.' In his present mood he was frightening.

'I saw your face in the water,' he said more quietly. 'You weren't just exhausted, you look sad-dened to death.'

'I'm sorry I gave you such a fright,' she said. '*All* of you. Everyone was so happy.'

'But you,' he said harshly. 'There's something disturbing your mind. Whatever it is, you must tell me.'

'There's nothing, Drew.'

'God, why aren't we married?' he burst out ex-plosively.

'Are you sure that's what you want?' The salty tears spilled over.

'Very sure,' he said, and his voice was hard and grim.

Carol rang the next day to make sure she had completely recovered from her fright.

'I've never seen Drew so tense and upset. It's very easy to see he loves you.'

And maybe he does, Marnie thought later, but as soon as he's away from me, he can't resist an intrigue. Sometimes, it seemed to her, women were mere pawns.

'Such a surprise!' Didi told her when she came back from the afternoon exercising. 'Mrs Drum-mond rang and she wants Davey and me along to the party.'

'Libby's party?' Marnie asked, frowning.

'Well, your dad is Mr Drummond's trainer.'
Didi's bright pleasure was somewhat dispelled.

'It's only recently she's condescended to speak
to us,' Marnie pointed out in a very dry voice.

'Who cares?' said Didi cheerfully. 'It gives us the
opportunity to dress up. Formal, she said.'

'It'd have to be,' Marnie muttered, but Didi
never even heard.

The Saturday of Libby Drummond's party,
Drew's brilliant three-year-old filly, Golden Rhapsody, former best two-year-old of the year, caused
a sensation when she finished an incredible eighth
in the sixteen-hundred-metre Classic, one of the
richest races of the Winter Carnival.

'She should have made mincemeat out of them!'
Dave ranted. 'A class horse like that!'

It was obvious the filly's owner thought so too,
and the top jockey, the flamboyant Darryl Bell,
had to endure an embarrassing ordeal when the
naturally disappointed punters let loose.

All in all it created a terrific buzz.

'In my opinion the . . . didn't try,' said Tiny, and
as he wouldn't dream of applying such a word to a
champion racehorse, it had to be the jockey.

An enquiry was later held and Bell, who usually
thrilled the crowd with a superb ride, maintained
that 'the horse was worked out.'

This, too, Dave received with contempt, reacting
as if the failure of his old favourite was his own
personal tragedy. Earlier on, one of Dave's stable

had pulled away to win an extremely tough sprint, but this didn't seem to compensate for Golden Rhapsody's dismal run.

'I'm sure Charlie knew something about it,' Didi hissed in Marnie's ear.

'*What?*' Marnie swung on her stepmother so vehemently, Didi retreated with shocked blue eyes.

'Charlie. Charlie Kingston,' Didi explained.

'I know that.' Marnie got a grip on Didi's arm. 'How come you and Charlie Kingston are so close?'

'Why, I bet with him all the time.'

'You talk too much, Dee,' Marnie said slowly, narrowing her eyes. 'So, apparently, does Charlie.'

'You know racing,' Didi tried to pass it off. 'You never know what's going to happen next.'

Marnie just looked back at her, temporarily robbed of the powers of speech. So Charlie Kingston had known Golden Rhapsody was not going to win? No matter what she thought it had to be left to the stewards to take action. Like her father, Marnie's whole life was filled with the love and admiration of horses. Very seldom did either of them bother about a gamble or indeed patronise Charlie Kingston, Didi's favourite bookmaker. Charlie's big handsome ruddy face came sharply to Marnie's mind. He had been placed beside Didi at the Cup dinner, frankly ogling her where he should not. Big, bluff, genial Charlie—the big-time bookmaker, and a lady's man.

Dave O'Connor kept talking about the sensation the whole time he was dressing (under protest) for Libby's twenty-first.

'Those moneymaking bookies cleaned it up! The best three-year-old in Australia not given a single opportunity to stretch out.'

'Forget it, honey!' Didi said earnestly, having made a small fortune.

'You know damn well these things affect me,' Dave returned irritably. 'Don't think I'll allow that yarn about her not being able to take the pressure. Golden Rhapsody is a champion, and you can't keep champions down.'

'Maybe she won't fail at her next start,' said Didi.

Already, thought Marnie, in the know, then immediately regretted the thought. Didi looked stunning, a beautiful blonde bombshell, but Dave regarded his delicious wife with a wince.

'Do you *have* to show your bosom?' he said crossly.

'What do you suggest I do with it, honey?' Didi turned back to the mirror studying her petite, shapely figure complacently. 'I know what's just right.'

'At any rate, that lecherous Kingston won't be there tonight.' Dave straightened up to smile. 'Honestly, he's the worst. . . .'

'How do I look?' Marnie changed the subject.

'Like a princess!' said Dave, telling the exact truth. Always a very pretty girl, nowadays Marnie's looks were positively blazing. *McIvor*, he thought, torn between possessiveness and pleasure. He had always had a special regard for the man, never dreaming he would take his darling daughter.

Leaving within minutes of each other, they all arrived together at the magnificent colonial-era house, Mayfield, that had been restored to its former glory as *the* venue for wedding receptions and large parties.

'I bet this cost them a packet!' Dave observed.

'Two hundred and sixty-four guests, I believe,' Drew put a steering hand under Marnie's elbow.

'At about thirty-four bucks a head!' Dave's face puckered wryly.

'That makes nine thousand two hundred and forty dollars!' said Didi, clacking it out like a cash register.

There was an instant of fraught silence, then Drew asked pleasantly, 'Can you do that again, Deirdre?'

'Sure, any time!' Didi gave him a brilliant smile. 'I don't even know how I do it, the answer just lights up in my brain.'

'It must come in very useful,' he said dryly.

'You'd think so,' Didi answered with a faint flicker of resentment, 'but Davey won't let me do the books any more.'

'Surely that's the Sorrensons arriving?' Marnie hurried forward so precipitously she nearly lost her footing.

'Why, I think it is.' Didi screwed up her short-sighted eyes. 'Gosh, isn't she skinny!'

'Don't say anything, *please*,' Marnie begged her sardonic fiancé as her father and Didi moved forward to greet the well known racing family.

'So it was Didi all along,' Drew murmured. 'God Almighty!'

'At last you know, and I don't want you to,' Marnie said in anguish. What she felt for Didi was close to what she would feel for an errant sister. 'She truly doesn't mean any harm.'

'She just believes a rich man is fair game.'

'Something like that,' Marnie said lamely. 'Don't challenge her, Drew. I couldn't bear to see her humiliated. She's so soft underneath, she'd just crumble.'

'It can't be any fun for your father.'

'He'll watch her from now on. In fact, he's driving himself mad.' Marnie's large velvety eyes were pleading. 'Please, Andrew!'

'What else could I do?' he seemed lost in thought. 'It shocked me to think it was Dave, but never for a moment did I consider Deirdre!'

'I told you,' she said miserably.

'My God! Poor old Dave, he would never have given her away.'

'He loves her,' said Marnie, watching her father stand talking, with his arm around Didi's waist. 'She only did it in the first place for her family. As it often happens, she gets to talking to people and they give her ideas. That rogue Jack Johnston for a start.'

'And Charlie Kingston for another.'

A point which had already occurred to Marnie.

'Shall we go in?' he asked dryly.

'Of course you're upset.' Marnie looked up at

his handsome, dark face.

'I won't argue with that.'

'I love you,' she said, because she couldn't help it.

'Cut it out, baby, I can't stand it.' In the garden lights, his eyes glittered over her like diamonds.

'I *do*,' she whispered, distraught.

'Hell, we don't have to go to this party,' he said with subdued violence.

'Why, it's expected,' she faltered, feelings building up in her, too-dominant feelings that threatened to swamp her.

'I want to love you, Marnie,' he sighed, all his cool suaveness gone. 'You obsess me.'

Behind them, Mrs Drummond sailed out on to the verandah.

'Why, Drew ... Marnie!' She extended her arms.

Such effusion was understandable, Marnie thought, going forward. Mrs Drummond loved mixing with the best people, and so long as she was with Drew, she was that.

It came then as no shock to see Liane Maxwell and her mother and father among the two hundred and sixty-four guests. Liane, with burning blue eyes devouring Drew wherever he went.

She's not over it at all, Marnie thought sadly. The very sight of him is enough to make her forget everything. And why not? Didn't he arouse the same feelings in herself?

It was the first time Marnie had been inside the lovely old house and Drew took her arm, pointing out architectural features. After that, everything seemed to merge into a blaze of light and laughter and chatter. Libby, looking flower-like in a beautiful white dress, welcomed Marnie warmly and planted a real kiss on Drew's tanned cheek. She looked the picture of innocence, but Marnie saw the flash of hunger in her china-blue eyes. There was no doubt about it; Drew had a great appeal for all women.

'Marnie, how beautiful you look!' Ross, who had been holding back until Drew was distracted, surged forward. 'I love your dress. Is it specially for the occasion?'

'Of course.' He had his hand on her arm, so she was obliged to go with him.

'You'll see Liane Maxwell in time, I doubt not,' he told her. 'One can scarcely offend the Judge.'

'Spoken like a true lawyer,' Marnie said lightly.

'God, I've missed you,' he sighed gustily.

'There are other girls in the world.'

'Not with red hair and dark eyes and skin like a pearl.'

'Come now,' she teased him. 'What's wrong with blonde hair and blue eyes?'

'You laid a spell on me, Marnie,' he maintained, looking a bit tragic.

'Fear not, I'll lift it,' she said kindly. 'Or Melissa will see to it that I do.'

'She's nice enough,' Ross's face was working in a curious way, 'but she's not you. Come over here, where I can have you to myself.'

'But Ross——' Marnie began, then shrugged

her delicate bare shoulders. If he wanted to get it out of his system, why not?

Several hectic hours later, Marnie put her champagne glass down and sought the fresh air. Drew had temporarily disappeared, but as he had never left her side, she had little cause for complaint.

Along the wide cool verandahs that enclosed the mansion on three sides, little groups were standing, the light splashing on the lovely colours of the women's dresses, the glitter of jewels. Her own dress had been carefully chosen by Didi and her old pal Jilly and put into Marnie's arms as another present. It was a very romantic dress, almost in the Scarlett O'Hara tradition—bare shoulders, low bodice, tiny waist and a wonderful bouffant skirt. An extravagant dress in a dull gold and one Jilly fully expected to draw in the customers.

Half way down the most secluded section of verandah, Marnie heard a low voice.

'How can you show me such cruelty?'

It was an impassioned woman's voice and one she easily recognised.

'Please, Liane, I'm very weary of this.'

Of course it was Drew.

Marnie stood stock still, all flush of excitement dying. Not for anything could she have moved from the spot, not even when she knew listening could bring her nothing but pain.

'Don't you remember all the good times we had together?' A bitter little laugh beset Liane.

'We were two people who came hopefully together,' he told her, 'but it didn't work out.'

'It did for me!'

'Then I'm sorry,' he had himself under control. 'I had no desire to hurt you, Liane, and I have none now.'

'I can't believe it's over!' Liane cried, while Marnie stood there appalled. 'We had so much!'

'Did we really?' His voice was gentle, but unutterably remote. 'There were many things on which our minds didn't touch. We didn't have the same sense of humour, or indeed the same interests. We didn't even like the same people. I'm a man who wants children, whereas you don't seem to like them.'

'It's possible to have a good marriage without children,' Liane burst out tempestuously. 'Is that why you're marrying the O'Connor girl? Let me tell you, that wilful little baggage will lead you a dance!'

'I've no doubt she will!' For the first time there was life and amusement in Drew's deep voice. 'No, in Marnie's case, Liane, it's the same old story. I love her.'

There was only Liane's sharp cry, then the sound of someone hurrying away.

It will take a while for this to sink in, Marnie thought, her knees crumpling under her.

'Why, Marnie!' Drew came on her, the light glinting on her red-gold hair.

'I was listening in to your quarrel,' she turned her almond gaze on him. Her voice trembled.

'I hope my part pleased you?' he asked a little roughly. Her skirt was spread out all around her and she looked beautiful, heartbreakingly young and literally unapproachable.

'You saw her in Sydney, didn't you?'

'Oh, Marnie,' he said, and sank down on the chair near her.

'Does love mean to you what it means to me?' she asked tragically.

'I don't deserve this,' he groaned.

'Go on,' she turned to him. 'Tell me about Sydney.'

'*Everything?*' he suddenly laughed.

'It's no laughing matter!' She spoke rather like Grandma O'Connor again.

'When I left you, Marnie, you were everything on my mind. You were *there*, and you still are. Think about it, darling, because you'll have to live with it.'

'And Liane?'

'Liane is one of those people who thinks persistence wins the day. She did give me one or two embarrassing moments, but I wasn't going to pass them on to you. It would hardly have been fair to upset you unnecessarily.'

'You didn't consider someone else might give me the story in colourful detail?' she asked tartly.

'Darling,' he said patiently, 'may I be absolutely frank?'

'I'm looking forward to it.'

'Trust me,' he said quietly. 'In your heart you know what we've got—a miracle. I love you, I long for you. I've waited for you all my life. I don't foresee the slightest difficulty in remaining faithful to you all my days. I'm not a promiscuous man, never have been. I'm a man who thought a deep, abiding love would go past him. That's why I call you my miracle.' He had been looking out over the garden, now he turned his head. 'You're crying.' His voice shook with emotion.

'Can't we go home?'

'Of course we can!' He got up and swept her to her feet. 'People simply accept it of engaged couples.'

'Whenever you go away again, I'm going to come with you,' Marnie told him. 'I love you so much it hurts me.'

With so many interested eyes on them, he could only glance down at her brilliantly. 'I'm going to make everything come right for all of us, Marnie. I swear it. You're all the world to me, and more.'

Dave, becoming anxious, had started to look for them, but when he saw them standing together on the verandah, Marnie's hand firmly in Drew's, her lovely young face glowing, he felt moved to a few tears of his own. The aura of love and pride around Drew was so great it was palpable, and when they turned together and saw him, waiting so quietly, they both smiled.

Dave felt his own heart lurch with love. They had a future. All of them. It was his turn now to go forward and congratulate them with all his heart.

THE ORIGIN OF THE THOROUGHBRED

In *The McIvor Affair,* Marnie's father is a trainer of
Thoroughbreds—race horses. Although the origin of this
magnificent breed would make a book in itself, we shall
impart to you here a little information on the subject.

Several hundred years ago, Thoroughbred horses did
not exist. In England at the time, there were only two kinds
of horses: large powerful steeds used by the cavalry, and
small, pony-sized, ordinary-looking horses that didn't
gallop, but paced; that is, both front and hind legs of the
right side would strike out in unison, to be followed by
front and hind legs of the left.

But then the situation began to change. At different
times in the early eighteenth century, three wealthy
Englishmen introduced to their homeland three dainty,
fleet-footed Arab stallions. When these animals were bred
with the English mares, an amazing thing happened: the
offspring were strong, streamlined and long of limb—and
dazzlingly swift.

Gradually the descendants of the three Arab stallions
filtered to the rest of Europe, North America and
Australia. Today, jockey clubs throughout the world define
Thoroughbreds as horses whose ancestry may be traced to
one of these three original Arabian sires.

4 FREE
Harlequin Romances